Lulu Atlantis

AND THE QUEST FOR TRUE BLUE LOVE

Lulu
Atlantis
AND
THE
QUEST
FOR
TRUE
BLUE
LOVE

by **Patricia Martin** Illustrated by **Marc Boutavant**

schwartz & wade books · new york

Text copyright © 2008 by Patricia Martin
Illustrations copyright © 2008 by Marc Boutavant

All rights reserved.
Published in the United States by Schwartz & Wade Books, an imprint of Random House
Children's Books, a division of Random House, Inc., New York.

"Pick Yourself Up" by Jerome Kern (music) and Dorothy Fields (lyrics) © 1936.
Used by Permission of Universal PolyGram International Publishing, Inc./ASCAP and
Happy Aspen Music LLC.
All Rights Reserved. International Copyright Secured.

Schwartz & Wade Books and colophon are trademarks of Random House, Inc.

www.randomhouse.com/kids

Educators and librarians, for a variety of teaching tools,
visit us at www.randomhouse.com/teachers

Library of Congress Cataloging-in-Publication Data

Martin, Patricia (Patricia A.)
Lulu Atlantis and the quest for true blue love / Patricia Martin. — 1st ed.
p.   cm.
Summary: Lulu Atlantis is peeved when her mother brings home little brother Sam, and she
turns to her imaginary friend, Harry the daddy long-legs spider, for comfort, companionship, help,
and advice as she is getting used to the addition to the family.
ISBN 978-0-375-84016-6 (trade) – ISBN 978-0-375-94016-3 (lib. bdg.)
[1. Brothers and sisters—Fiction.   2. Jealousy—Fiction.   3. Imaginary playmates—Fiction.
4. Spiders—Fiction.]   I. Title.
PZ7.M364165Lul 2008
[Fic]—dc22   2007002082

The text of this book is set in Belen and Rosanna Script.
The illustrations are rendered in Adobe Photoshop.
Book design by Rachael Cole

Printed in the United States of America

10 9 8 7 6 5 4 3 2 1

First Edition

For S.A.M. with love
—P.M.

part one
The Gathering of Friends

CHAPTER ONE

The day her mother returned from the hospital to their house on Sweet Pea Lane was the day Lulu Atlantis ran away from home.

The first place she ran was beneath the baby grand piano in the living room. She crawled under, curled up on the rug and listened to the turmoil coming from the back of the house.

"I can still hear that racket at the back of the house," Lulu told Harry. Harry was her best friend. He lived under the piano.

"What racket?" asked Harry.

"*That* racket! The singing!"

"The singing, miss? How can a lullaby be a racket?" asked Harry.

"Not to even mention that *snuffling*. That *huffing!*"

"Do you mean the tiny, soft, cuddly sound a baby makes when he's sleeping?" asked Harry, primping his red bow tie.

"*That's* the racket I'm talking about!" said Lulu.

"Oh, my," murmured Harry, rolling his eyes.

"Obviously, under the piano is not far away enough," Lulu said.

Harry took off the black top hat he always wore

and, with the cuff of one of his many green sleeves, brushed off its crown.

"Well, you know what I always tell you. Go where life takes you. So where do you propose we go?" Harry asked Lulu. He passed his hat from one hand to the other to the other to the other to the other. Being a daddy longlegs spider, he had many hands to pass his hat to. Then he patted it back into place on his head and looked at his face in one of the shining brass piano pedals that hung suspended over the Persian carpet. Harry often looked at his face in shiny surfaces. He was a reflective sort of spider.

Lulu rubbed her chin. "Hmmmm. I'm thinking . . . I'm thinking," she said. "I've got it! I propose we run away to . . . the Umbrella Tree!" she cried.

"The Umbrella Tree has always been a place of great comfort to us when we are down and out," Harry said. "Close enough not to wear out our feet, yet far away enough not to hear any racket." Harry nodded. "The Umbrella Tree it is."

Lulu picked Harry up. She slid him easily into the buttoned pocket of her smock. Then she crawled out from under the piano and stood up.

"Hold on a minute," Harry said, poking his head out of the pocket. He scrambled over the pocket's edge and down Lulu's pant leg.

Harry joggled over to one of the brass piano pedals. A sugar cookie shaped like a spider sat on it. He dragged the cookie off the pedal and placed it at the toe of Lulu's sneaker.

"You'll need this," he said as he scrambled up Lulu's leg and into her smock pocket once again.

"What for?" said Lulu.

"You'll see."

Lulu shrugged, bent down, picked up the cookie and slipped it into her pocket, alongside the spider.

"Lately, Harry, you're taking better care of me than Mother is."

"That's perfectly understandable, given the circumstances," said Harry. "Mother has other fish to fry."

"Hmmmmm," said Lulu. "Some fish!"

Before going out the front door, Lulu leaned over to look back into the nursery, to where her mother sat curled in a rocking chair, snuggled inside a fluffy blue robe. She was rocking and singing a lullaby.

"I can see I'm not needed around here!" said Lulu. She kicked the front door open with her foot and slammed it shut with a twist of her hip.

CHAPTER TWO

Lulu checked her pocket. She could see Harry reclining against its seam, and she could hear him whistle as she toted him down the slope of the front lawn.

Lulu plowed through the tall green grass that stood in its eternal wait for Father to come home to mow it. She stomped around half-buried boulders that cast lumpish shadows in the yellow afternoon light, past red geraniums in their urns and the pink hummingbird garden and Mother's newborn pumpkin patch. She didn't stop for a breath until she got all the way down to the bottom of the lawn, where the Umbrella Tree stood in a pool of its own light.

Please understand, the Umbrella Tree was not a tree as most people would imagine a tree to be. It was a large mulberry tree made of branches that hung down to the ground, which made it look like a giant umbrella. The branches sprouted glossy green leaves and were studded with luscious purple berries.

As Lulu crawled through the branches, sticky curtains of wispy stuff stuck to her in tatters.

"Ugh!" said Lulu, picking strands from her shoulders and out of her hair. "What's all this?"

"*This* is my web, and *you've* ruined it!" said a harsh voice. "And not only that, you've disturbed my baby!"

Lulu looked up into the branches. A spider as big as a soup bowl peered down at her with red eyes and a ghastly grimace. In several of the spider's hairy arms lay an equally hairy, black little bundle. The baby spider opened its mouth and bawled. The mother spider hissed at Lulu.

"Harry! Is that a relative?" whispered Lulu.

"No relative of mine!" whispered Harry. He gulped and shuddered and pulled at his starched collar. He crept to the deepest depths of Lulu's pocket.

"*Out . . . of . . . my . . . house!*" the spider hissed. "*Or I'll . . .*"

Keeping her eyes on Lulu, the spider set her tiny bundle between two leaves on a branch. She crept on tiptoes (many of them: pit-pat-pit-pat-pit) across the branch, bearing down on Lulu.

Lulu shook in her shoes. She backed up an inch,

then another inch, then hit the wall of tree branches behind her and couldn't move any farther.

The spider crouched . . . she sprang . . . she pounced!

Poor Lulu! "Help!" she shouted.

Pressing herself down flat, Lulu pushed with all her might and squeezed out from under the Umbrella Tree's branches.

"It's a miracle I'm not squished flat!" Harry cried, crawling out of Lulu's pocket, coughing and gasping for breath.

"This is a fine kettle of fish!" said Lulu, standing up, feeling braver out in the sunshine. "I'm out of a home *and* a hiding place!" She placed her fists on her hips and gave the tree the eye. "Oh, well, Harry. The Umbrella Tree would never have worked as a place to run away to, anyway. I can *still* hear that racket from the back of the house!"

"Not to mention the racket from inside the Umbrella Tree," said Harry. He cupped one hand to his ear, listening to the mother spider screeching an ugly lullaby to quiet her ugly baby.

"We have to move on, Harry."

"There's no avoiding it, I fear," said Harry. "But at least take these, miss." He held one berry in each of his hands and dropped them into Lulu's palm one by one.

Lulu pocketed the berries alongside the spider cookie, which had miraculously survived her roll out of the spider's den in one piece.

"Why do I need all this stuff?" Lulu said.

"You are gathering souvenirs to give to someone you love when you return home," said Harry.

"I'll never return home! And I don't love *anyone* at the moment, thank you very much!" said Lulu.

"No one?" said Harry.

"No one."

Harry shook his head, shrugged his many shoulders and climbed back into her pocket. "Which way?" he asked.

"That way," said Lulu, pointing directly down Sweet Pea Lane. She looked back over her shoulder toward the house. She saw that no one was watching. Not even Mother. Lulu swung herself away from the house so sharply, a fly zimming by was knocked unconscious in midflight.

CHAPTER THREE

Lulu and Harry journeyed down Sweet Pea Lane. They passed Farmer Wallenhaupt's raspberry patch. They traveled under birds' nests and followed the lemon sun to Farmer Wallenhaupt's Frog Pond. When they got there, Lulu looked back toward home.

"I don't see anybody looking for me," she said. "And I can still hear that racket."

"Are you sure, miss? I can't hear a thing from this distance," Harry said. He whistled, rolled his eyes to the sky and played with the fingertips of his white gloves.

"Hmpfff!" said Lulu, and then she turned her attention to Farmer Wallenhaupt's Frog Pond.

Please understand, Farmer Wallenhaupt's Frog Pond was not a pond as most people would imagine a pond to be. It was filled with silver water whose droplets slid about like mercury. This was a frog pond in which tadpoles turned into butterflies and water witches turned into clumps of wild roses. Frogs sang arias from *Madama Butterfly* while playing swamp hockey along the pond's edge. Dragonflies dusted with glitter hovered overhead like the helicopters of fairies. It was for all these lovely reasons that Farmer Wallenhaupt guarded his Frog Pond as if it were a sacred treasure.

The old man Wallenhaupt was a fierce guard. Having no children of his own, he had no patience with them, and he certainly had no sense of humor. Children the region over were terrified at the very thought of him. Babysitters who could not get children to go to bed at night said to them, "Okay then, I'll have Farmer

Wallenhaupt come put you to bed!" And the children would dive under the covers. Parents who could not get their children to do their chores said to them, "Fine. I'm calling Farmer Wallenhaupt! Here I go!" And the children would jump to their jobs and finish them in a minute flat. The citizens of the region were in no need of the boogeyman. They had Farmer Wallenhaupt.

Both Lulu Atlantis and Harry were well aware of his threat.

"Any interesting frogs to catch?" Harry asked, trying to appear nonchalant. But inside, he was praying that there weren't any. Harry did not want to incur the wrath of Farmer Wallenhaupt, nor did he want to share his pocket today. Frogs tended to smell like swamps, and they were usually rude, to boot.

"I suppose," said Lulu.

"You suppose *yes,* or you suppose *no?*" said Harry.

"I suppose it doesn't matter," said Lulu.

In an attempt to divert Lulu's attention away from frogs, Harry said, "Some welcome home you gave Mother, miss."

"Whose side are you on, anyway?" asked Lulu, eyeing the pond for prey.

Harry shrugged his many shoulders. They looked like waves in the ocean. "It's a big house you live in. Always room for one more, I'd say," said Harry, now trying to get his shoulders to stop at the same time.

"What does she need one more for, when she's got *me*? I thought she and me had a special thing going here, especially when Father is away on his crusades. There's *Mother* and there's *me*. She and me, me and she, thick as thieves and that is that! Isn't that what True Blue Love is, Harry? Just two?"

"Well . . . ," Harry began, but Lulu didn't wait for an answer.

"And then she goes and brings this . . . this . . . this . . . *him* . . . home!" Lulu scratched at her head furiously, even though it didn't itch. She took a stone and threw it hard at the helpless water.

"I don't think there is any limit on True Blue Love. The more the merrier, I say," said Harry.

"Yeah, yeah, yeah," Lulu murmured, pitching another stone into the water.

"Ribbit," said a nearby frog.

The nearby frog was quite the chap, portly and brilliantly green and mildly cross-eyed. About his rotund middle he wore a golden belt that glinted in the sunlight.

Lulu lunged at the frog. He sidestepped her and she fell flat on her face in the dirt.

"Better watch out, Miss Lulu. Farmer Wallenhaupt might be on the prowl. I hear he carries an axe, just in case he comes across any frog hunters. Or children," said Harry.

"Farmer Wallenhaupt is no match for Lulu

Atlantis!" said Lulu, getting up and lunging at the frog again.

"Hah!" she cried. "Gotcha! I've been trying to get this one for weeks, Harry. *This* is my Frog Prince!"

Harry eyed the frog's mildly crossed eyes and the golden belt about his rotund middle. Harry said, "If that's your Frog Prince, I'd say his crown has slipped somewhat."

Lulu shoved the frog into her smock pocket. Harry crawled in too, to keep an eye on him. "Behave yourself," said Harry testily. "Watch where you sit. Don't squash the berries. Don't eat the cookie."

"Ribbit," said the frog.

"HEY! YOU THERE! PUT MY FROG BACK WHERE YOU FOUND IT!" roared an ill-spirited voice. The voice boomed out of the grouchy-looking mouth on the grouchy-looking face of grouchy Farmer Wallenhaupt.

Harry popped his head out. "There he is! He's got the axe! Make a run for it!"

Farmer Wallenhaupt did not have an axe, but he did have a rake. As he ran at Lulu, he waved the rake in the air over his head. "I'M TELLIN' YOUR MOTHER ON YOU, I AM! YOU . . . YOU . . . *KID!*"

"Holy Toledo!" cried Lulu and Harry at the same time.

Harry ducked back down into Lulu's pocket. Lulu spun and ran as fast as she could, zooming out onto Sweet Pea Lane, then darting down it farther than she had ever been before.

CHAPTER FOUR

Lulu ran and ran until she could run no more. She stopped, gasping for breath. She leaned over and cupped her knees with her hands. When she finally stood up and looked behind her, Farmer Wallenhaupt was nowhere in sight. In fact, the road was frighteningly empty. Not a bird, not a grasshopper, not even a gnat was about.

And for the very first time, Lulu could no longer see her house. Suddenly, the strings that wound around her heart tightened, tugging her back in the direction of home.

Doubts crept into her mind. The doubts whispered to Lulu: *Is this safe? What are you doing? You can only be headed for trouble!*

But Lulu would have none of these doubts! "Mind your own business, Heart! Keep a stout heart, Mind!" she said aloud. "We're not going back!"

"Who are you talking to?" called Harry.

"Nobody!"

Harry peeped his head out. Frog Prince's head peeped out behind Harry's.

"All clear, miss?" Harry whispered, peering down the road behind them.

"All clear. Oh, well, Harry. We had to leave the frog pond anyway. I could still hear that racket at the back of the house," Lulu said.

"You must have twenty-twenty hearing, miss," said Harry, looking at her doubtfully.

"I do, Harry, I do."

"It's getting late, you know, miss," said Harry. "It's getting cold. And it's gotten very dark in this pocket lately."

"Ribbit," said the frog.

"We'll camp out," said Lulu.

"Camp out? You mean, out as in *outside?*" asked Harry.

"Where else? The wide-open spaces," said Lulu, spinning like a top and flinging her arms wide to encompass all outdoors.

"The exposed, cold, lost and lonely wide-open spaces? With no room service?" asked Harry.

"Get a grip, Harry," said Lulu.

Lulu took several tentative steps down the road, then stopped.

"Do you know where we are?" she whispered.

"No. Do you?" Harry whispered back.

"No."

Harry, staying securely in the smock pocket, turned his head to look up the road and down. Frog Prince did the same.

Harry said quietly, "Which way is home?"

"Forget home. We *have* no home," said Lulu in a low, angry voice. "We're going to venture on, as adventurers would do. As *Father* would do! We'll show them!"

"But Mother will worry," said Harry.

"Let her."

They stood alone under the vast, empty sky, on the endless, empty road.

Finally Harry whispered, "Which way, then?"

"I . . . I guess . . . (gulp) . . . that way," said Lulu, chewing her fingertips.

The sun yawned. Its warm lemon light was turning slowly to the cold pewter of twilight.

They journeyed down the lane, through wind and through shadow. They passed the dens of sharp-toothed foxes and the caves of hungry bears and the possible lair of a possible lion. Lulu shuddered.

"You do realize, don't you, Harry, that all this is entirely Mother's fault?" Lulu said, talking as they walked. She held her arms close across her chest, trying not to shudder anymore.

Harry didn't answer.

"Not to even mention *you-know-who!*"

Harry didn't answer again.

"And Father going off on another crusade certainly doesn't help," said Lulu, tightening her arms even closer across her chest.

"Father is off to save the Pacific Northwest Tree Octopus, miss. It is a worthy crusade and a worthy cause. Father loves his worthy causes," said Harry.

"Actually, I think he is saving the Double-Eyed Fig Parrot this time," said Lulu.

Harry looked up at Lulu. "Double-Eyed Fig Parrot?" he said. "Well, whatever Father is saving this time, he still loves *you*, miss."

"Some love."

"Father is out there saving the Double-Eyed Fig Parrot, and at the same time gathering adventure stories to tell you when he comes home. He knows how you love his stories, Lulu Atlantis," said Harry.

"Yes, well, that's true. I do love Father's stories," Lulu murmured. She stopped at the edge of the dark woods.

"Have we found a camping place?" Harry asked.

Lulu said nothing.

A sound drifted toward them. It was the sound of a lonely soul lost in a lonely wood.

"Did you hear that?" whispered Harry, his voice shaking.

"No! And neither did you!" said Lulu. She spoke sharply, but at the same time, she gently put her hand in her pocket, scooped Harry up and held on tight.

"We're going into those woods and settle for the night!" said Lulu. "And that is *that!*"

Please understand, the woods that lined that particular road were not woods as most people would imagine woods to be. They blocked out what light there was so that there was no color to be seen, only grays and blacks. The trees were mired to their knees in slimy mud. Their branches looked like the wings of vampire bats. Here witches did not turn into clumps of wild roses. They remained as witches, with warts, hair wriggling like worms, and gray, rotted teeth. There were no glittering dragonflies, only mud wasps and unhappy slithering things. These woods were as bleak as a midwinter midnight. Poor Lulu! Poor Harry! Poor Frog Prince!

Lulu wandered slowly through the woods until she came to a spot where the forest floor was level and relatively free of jagged roots. The ground was covered by pine needles, and the view of the sky was covered by tall pine trees.

"We'll stay here," said Lulu. She gathered up pine needles into a long pile like a mattress. She thumped herself down flat, lying straight as a statue, and stretched her legs out until they snapped tight. She crisscrossed her arms over her chest.

Harry and Frog Prince climbed stiffly out of the pocket, looking first one way and then the other. Frog Prince hopped up close to Harry and wrapped his green arms tightly around Harry's tiny brown body. Harry's eyes and Frog Prince's eyes were wide and white in the dim light.

"*This* is where we're staying, miss?" gulped Harry.

"Yes! Wanna make something of it?" snapped Lulu. She pressed her crisscrossed arms down hard over her chest. "Pipe down," she whispered to her pounding heart.

"I can't see any sky with these stupid trees in the way," she said more loudly. "Mother *loves* trees. Personally, *I* think there're far too many in the world."

"It is indeed unfortunate that you can't see any sky through the treetops," said Harry, trying to extricate himself from Frog Prince's grip. "At home, you can just look through your window and *voilà!* There is the sky!"

"Sure. If you can *get* to the window with all the piles of diapers and baby bottles in the way!" said Lulu. She screwed up her face. "I have to go to the bathroom. There's no bathroom out here!"

"Indeed," said Harry. "When you were at home, you had a nice bathroom. With seashells and fluffy, warm towels and the color lavender."

Frog Prince nodded in agreement, being too frightened to even ribbit.

"Are you hungry, Harry?" asked Lulu.

"Who could possibly eat under these circumstances?" he asked.

"Eating makes everything better, Mother always says. How about the cookie?"

"You will need the cookie later, for a gift," said Harry. "And the same thing applies to the berries, just in case you're thinking about the berries."

"How about the *frog*?" said Lulu. She was feeling particularly mean at the moment.

"Ribbit!" screamed the frog. He jumped a foot in the air, releasing Harry so violently that Harry was flung to the ground.

Frog Prince hopped helter-skelter though the trees, all the way back to Farmer Wallenhaupt's Frog Pond.

"My Frog Prince!" cried Lulu. She sat up and clutched her hands to her heart.

"Your Frog Prince has flown the coop. So much for frog princes," said Harry.

"Some relationships just don't hold water." Lulu stood up. "C'mon," she said.

"Where to, miss?" asked Harry.

"I don't know, Harry. I just don't know!" Her throat constricted and her eyes burned. She put her fists on her hips and held her chin up high in an attempt to appear brave.

"There's always home," suggested Harry.

"When certain people are brought home from the hospital, with no invitation whatsoever from certain other people, then home is too crowded," Lulu spat. (But she had to admit to herself, the sound of the word *home* was sweet to her ears.)

"Sam is your brother, miss," said Harry softly.

"Sam is one too many. Sam is a third wheel. Sam is . . . C'mon, Harry. We're moving on!" Lulu spun herself around and walked quickly away. She walked quickly away from Harry, and from the sweetness of the word *home*. She walked quickly away from the thought of the warmth of her kitchen on a winter's evening, from the thought of the softness of the pillows on her bed, and from the memory of the crisp, clean fragrance of Mother's perfume.

Hanging on to his top hat with one hand, Harry ran after her, catching the hem of her smock with a few other hands. He crawled deep into her pocket, shaking his head at the folly of his friend.

CHAPTER FIVE

Lulu's walk evolved into a trot, which became an out-and-out run. She had no idea where she was headed. She just *ran*. Tears welled in her eyes, blurring her vision. She tripped over a branch and then a root and then a rock. Lulu would not give in to actually *crying*—no actual *sobbing*. Just sniffling and snuffling and pushing at branches that snapped at her face and pulled at her hair. Twigs on the ground nipped her legs with their brittle teeth.

Harry squeezed his eyes shut and held on to the pocket seam for dear life.

Lulu came to a clearing in the trees, where a last patch of light sent a pale beam streaming into the darkness. She stopped short. In fact, she stopped so short, Harry was thrown flat against the front of the pocket. "Ouch!" he cried, and popped his head out to see what was going on.

In front of Lulu, in the streaming beam of left-over light, a skunk ran in circles. His head was stuck in an empty yogurt container with a picture of a cow on it. Around and around the skunk ran, shaking his head.

Lulu rubbed at her eyes, as if the tears in them might be causing her to hallucinate. "Am I *seeing things*?" she asked.

Harry looked at the skunk, and then at Lulu. "If you are, I am too! My, oh, my!" said Harry, looking bug-eyed at the skunk. "And you think *you* have it bad, miss!" he said to Lulu.

"I've heard enough from you, Harry," Lulu said, and buttoned up her pocket. Then she cried, "Hey! Hey, you! Skunk!"

The skunk stopped in his tracks and swung his yogurt container toward Lulu's voice.

"What are you doing?" asked Lulu.

"Mmmmmmmpfff mmmmmmmmpfff," replied the skunk.

Lulu crept over to the skunk and removed the yogurt container from his head, gently so as not to give him a scare. She put the container into one of her empty pockets. Then she bent down and said directly into the skunk's face, "I couldn't understand a thing you said."

"No kidding, with my head stuck in a yogurt container!" cried the skunk.

"So what did you say?"

"What I *said* was 'What does it look like?' "

"It looks like you're running in circles with an empty yogurt container stuck on your head," said Lulu.

"Precisely," said the skunk.

"Why?"

"Why are *you* running in circles *without* a yogurt container stuck on your head?" asked the skunk.

"You're a belligerent little fellow, aren't you?"

"Never make a skunk mad!" Lulu heard Harry calling from her pocket.

Harry pushed at the buttoned flap of Lulu's pocket until his head poked out. He nodded politely to the skunk, raised his crushed hat from his bruised noggin and said, "Top of the day to you."

"I'll give you the top of the day," the skunk said. "I'll give it to you right over the top of your head!" And then the skunk, pointing his finger at Lulu, said, "He's right, kid. Don't never make a skunk mad."

"HAH!" Lulu snapped. She poked the skunk in his soft belly with her finger, punctuating her words. "I'll give *you* something over *your* head, buddy! I've got a father who's always away, a mother who forgets I even exist, and an uninvited baby brother who hogs every minute of Mother's time! And I'm running far away to places I've never been before! I've got my hands full, buddy. And *you're* telling *me* not to make a *skunk* mad? HA HA! OOOoooooo . . . I'm so scared! I'm so scared I think I'll keel over!" And Lulu dropped down flat on the ground, playing dead.

"So? You think *that's* bad?" the skunk snapped right back at Lulu. "I get sideswiped by a wild fat frog tearing through the woods. He runs me down, does a flip-flop and a somersault, and this gold belt comes flying at me and crowns me smack on the head. I keel over on my keester and wouldn't you know wind up head-first in this empty yogurt container. And the yogurt's *peach*! I *hate* peach!"

"Well!" said Lulu, sitting up slowly. "Well . . . ," she said again, bending her knees up and resting her elbows on them. She held her head in her hands, collecting her thoughts and moaning.

While Lulu was holding her head and collecting her thoughts and moaning, the skunk turned to Harry. He asked in a hushed voice, "So what's the story with the kid? Where's her dad?"

Harry whispered back to the skunk, "Father is a great crusader. He goes on missions to save animals that are in danger of being wiped out."

"Like me with my head stuck in a yogurt container!" said the skunk.

"No, no, not like that. Like this. Suppose everybody hunts pretty purple birds for their pretty purple feathers to decorate hats and pillows. In time, there are no more pretty purple birds anywhere. They've all been wiped out. Father goes to put a stop to the wiping out of the animals."

"I got no problem with that," said the skunk.

"Neither do we. But it *does* mean that Father is away from home a lot," said Harry.

"Ahhh. Gotcha." The skunk looked over his shoulder at Lulu, who was still sitting and holding her head. He turned back to Harry. "Poor kid," he said. "And so what's with the new baby?"

"A bit of a surprise to us all, granted. But a most welcome surprise, I might add."

"Toots don't seem to think so," said the skunk, pointing with his thumb in her direction.

"Miss Lulu does not take well to change, I'm afraid," said Harry.

"Yeah, so . . . the world's tough all over," said the skunk. He was standing upright, his arms folded in front of him. He kicked carelessly at stones, sending several skimming across the ground. All of a sudden, one came whizzing back, jabbing him in his foot. He looked up to see Lulu kicking her way over to him and Harry.

"Hey!" yelped the skunk.

"Hey yourself," said Lulu. Then, ignoring his grimace, she continued, "Okay, I've got my thoughts together and this is what I think. Life is what it is. You got sideswiped by a frog. I got sideswiped by a family. So let's move on. Now, can you answer me this, please? Where am I? Where should I go? What should I do?"

Harry piped up. "I thought *I* was your answer guy."

Lulu gave Harry the eye.

"Look, girlie, I'm a skunk, not a magician. I don't got all the answers," said the skunk, scampering over to Lulu. He stood up on his hind legs and took her hand. He pressed something into it.

"The golden belt," said Lulu.

"Yeah, yeah, the golden belt," said the skunk. "It should bring *you* better luck than it brought me."

Lulu slipped the Frog Prince's golden belt onto her wrist.

"Here's something else, kiddo." The skunk reached down and picked up several smooth stones from the ground. He dropped them into Lulu's hand.

"Stones?" said Lulu.

"Yeah, stones. Like in your mother's garden."

"You know Mother's garden?" asked Lulu.

"Sweetheart, I know everything for miles around, believe you me. And I also know this . . . just rub them stones. You rub 'em an' make a wish and everything'll be okeydokey. Hunky-dory. A-OK," he said. "Got it, buttercup?"

"Will they bring me True Blue Love?" asked Lulu.

The skunk looked at Lulu. "Hah! That's a good one!"

And with that, the skunk turned his nose to the ground, sniffing out goodies for supper.

"Well, can you at least tell me where we've gotten ourselves to?" asked Lulu.

"Ya got yourselves close to where you wanna go, kiddo," said the skunk. "Ya got yourselves close to home."

"Home. Even if I *wanted* to go there, I'm a thousand miles away," said Lulu, chewing on her lower lip.

"A thousand miles? You gotta be kiddin', toots! Your house is a hop, skip and jump up the road! Just go that-away through those two white birch trees—you see those two white birch trees? Good. Go straight through them out to Sweet Pea Lane, then up the lane past the raspberry patch. Got it? Okay. Then go straight up Sweet Pea about twenty steps, turn left at the Umbrella Tree, go up your yard . . . and there you be!" said the skunk.

"There I be?" said Lulu.

"We're that close?" said Harry.

But the skunk, no fool for wasted time, had already headed out of the thin beam of light.

Lulu jumped up off the ground. "How do I know the stones will work?" she called after him.

The skunk turned to Lulu and called back, "It's all in the believing, sister." He saluted grandly, bowed and disappeared into the shadows of the trees.

Lulu looked at Harry. Harry looked at Lulu.

Harry said, "Stones. Just like in Mother's garden."

"So I heard," said Lulu. She rubbed the stones, clinking them together. They made a delicate, clean, almost musical *clink clink clink.*

"Home is a good place to go," continued Harry.

"I told you, home is too crowded," said Lulu.

"Give it a chance, miss. Everything in this world deserves a chance," said Harry.

Clink clink clink.

"Do you think Father will come home soon, Harry?" asked Lulu.

"It's hard to say."

"Well, if you *had* to say, what would you say?" said Lulu.

"I would say . . . perhaps it *is* all in the believing, miss. If you believe it will happen, it *will*."

Clink clink clink.

"Well, miss, what do you say? Where do we go from here?" asked Harry.

"I say . . . go where life takes you," said Lulu. "Where do you think life will take us now, Harry?"

"In my experience, life usually ends up taking you home," said Harry. "In my experience, home is where one needs to be at the end of a day."

Lulu scratched her head. She listened to the silent

loneliness of the woods. She felt the tugging of her heart's strings. She gave the stones another clink, then rubbed them until they were hot in her hand. She whispered, "Oh, stones, I wish for a sign that shows me the right place to go."

A breeze kicked up and tickled her ears and brought a sweet, crisp fragrance to her nose . . . a fresh, powdery, baby-skin-soft fragrance.

Lulu breathed deeply, inhaling the fragrant breeze. And then she said to Harry, "Well, maybe we *will* give it one chance. *One* chance."

Harry said in a voice soft with happiness, "Maybe one chance will be all we need."

"C'mon, Harry, we're going home."

"Hallelujah!"

"But just understand, mister, I'm doing this basically for *you*. You've done nothing but complain since we ran away!" said Lulu.

"Yes, miss."

"And never let it be said I let my friends down," added Lulu.

"Yes, miss."

They were silent for a while, feeling their way out of the woods and onto the road.

"The road to home looks good to me, and that is all I can say," said Harry.

And that *is* all that was said, all the way home.

CHAPTER SIX

Lulu tiptoed into the back of the house, where her mother nodded in the same rocking chair, with her eyes closed. The room had a baby-skin-soft fragrance that made Lulu feel glad she was there.

The room was dark, lit only by a small, amber light. The light illuminated the crib, and inside the crib lay a tiny being—a pint-sized version of Lulu Atlantis.

The tiny being looked up at Lulu through sleepy eyes. He yawned and smacked his lips.

Lulu looked down at Harry, who was settled on the toe of her shoe. "I don't know, Harry," she whispered.

"Go ahead," said Harry. He scuttled up the leg of her pants and jumped to the rail of the crib, where he could see Sam and still keep a sharp eye on Lulu.

Lulu said softly to the baby, "You're too little. You're too ugly."

Harry shook his head. "Not a promising start."

Sam whimpered.

Lulu tried again. "Okay, so maybe you're not so bad-looking. When you're not crying." Sam opened his tiny mouth into a tiny circle as if to say "Oooooh."

"Better," said Harry.

With the tip of her pinkie, Lulu touched Sam's hand. He grabbed her finger.

"He's holding on for dear life!" said Lulu.

"That's what babies do," said Harry.

"He's holding on to the wrong girl, if you ask me."

"Maybe yes, maybe no."

The baby gurgled and drizzled spit out of the side of his mouth.

"Yuck," said Lulu, wrinkling her nose.

Sam belched.

Squinting through the dim light, Lulu looked closely at the tiny face. "Something looks familiar," she said.

"Something should," said Harry. "After all, Sam's your brother."

"Hmmmmmmm," said Lulu, swinging the baby's fist about with her finger.

"Try the gifts," said Harry.

"The cookie's yours, Harry," Lulu said.

"What do I want with another cookie? I'm sweet enough." Harry grinned and batted his eyelashes.

Lulu frowned at Harry and Harry frowned back. He smiled. "Go ahead, miss."

Lulu shrugged and gently pulled her finger out of Sam's grip. "Well, I suppose the kid is here to stay."

"Ah, that he is, Miss Lulu Atlantis, that he is!" said Harry, delighted with Lulu's change of heart. He did a tap dance along the crib rail.

Lulu put the cookie close by Sam's head. This cookie, like the sun, warmed things up in friendship.

She put the berries in the empty yogurt container in the corner of the crib. The berries gave out a ripe, fruity fragrance.

Lulu showed Sam the gold Frog Prince belt. She brought his little hand to it and curled his fingers around the slim gold band. She held the belt in Sam's hand for him and waved his hand back and forth. The gold glinted in the dim light.

"So how do you think it's going, Harry?" Lulu said.

"I'd say it's going swimmingly," said Harry. "I would say that you are the Sister of Sam's Dreams."

"You think he knows who I am?"

"How could he not? What's more important than a big sister?" Harry said, then flipped himself off the side of the crib, scurried down Lulu's smock and settled himself into her pocket.

"I'm your big sister, mister," Lulu said, drawing the golden belt away from Sam and placing it on the little table beside his crib. "You'd better listen to me."

Lulu bent her head way down toward Sam's. She sort of smiled at him, and she sort of blew him a kiss. Then she quickly stood up and looked around, making sure no one had seen her sort of smile and sort of blow a kiss.

Lulu put the stones into the palm of her hand and held them up for Sam to see.

"My friend gave me these, mister. I'll hold on to them until you're old enough," Lulu told her brother.

"It's worth the wait. I'd say they've got at least two good wishes left to them. We'll share. Okay, kiddo?"

Sam's eyes twinkled.

Then Lulu heard Mother say, "Welcome back, Lulu Atlantis. You were missed. And so was your Harry."

Tucked away in the cozy nest of Lulu's pocket, Harry primped his red bow tie, gave his hat a good brush and settled in for the night.

part two
The Secret Ingredient

CHAPTER ONE

Mornings in the kitchen in summertime went like this: Mother opened the windows and the songs of birds flew in, sweeping across spice tins, blocks of baking chocolate and jars of honey and maple syrup. The songs were so sweet, they caused the very air to sparkle, as if Mother had taken sugar and thrown it about and it had suddenly stopped, suspended in air. Lulu Atlantis and Harry favored mornings in the kitchen in summertime.

Sam the Baby was now Sam the Toddler. His feet worked almost as well as his hands and knees to get him about. He toddled on tiptoes to his high chair and raised his arms up to Mother to be lifted into it.

Since Sam had begun to eat regular people food, Mother had taken to fixing everyone oatmeal for breakfast.

"After all, I'm not a short-order cook," said Mother brightly. "One pot for the family."

"I hate oatmeal. Where's my blueberry pancakes? Where's my bacon?" asked Lulu.

"Blueberry pancakes and bacon are too heavy for Sam's stomach. He's just a baby still," said Mother. She danced over to Sam, took his hands and kissed them, then touched the tip of his nose with the tip of her finger. "My little Sammy and his o-o-oatmeal!" she sang.

"Oh, sure. Let's make sure *Sam* gets everything *he* wants!" Lulu made a show of pushing her oatmeal aside.

Sam, on the other hand, gobbled down his oatmeal voraciously.

"At least *somebody's* happy," Lulu said to Harry, eyeing both Sam and Mother in a most unbecoming fashion.

"If looks could kill . . . ," said Harry.

"You might think about giving Mother a break from making breakfast, miss," said Harry one morning.

"Why? How hard is it to make *oatmeal*?" said Lulu.

"Oh, I don't know, miss," he said, whistling and looking at the ceiling.

"Well, *I* know! It's *easy*." Lulu crossed her arms over her chest in a definite and final manner.

"You know, miss, Mother might be more inclined to

fix blueberry pancakes and bacon if she had a bit of time off from fixing *him* breakfast," Harry said, tilting his top hat toward Sam.

Lulu cocked her head to one side. "Hmmm," she said, rubbing her chin. "You may be right, Harry. After all, Mother *is* getting on in years. She could use a break."

"Oh, yes, indeed," said Harry. "She is *indeed* getting on in years!" Harry looked at his reflection in the silver toaster and whistled.

So Lulu turned to Mother, who was washing up the breakfast dishes, and announced, "Mother, tomorrow I'll give Sam his breakfast. You need a break."

Mother turned and clasped her hands together under her chin and said, "A break! Why, Lulu Atlantis, a break is *exactly* what I need! Thank you so much. Tomorrow morning I shall remember to stay in bed and sleep the sleep of the deep. Why, maybe I'll stay in bed and sleep the sleep of the deep until lunchtime!"

"Yeah, well, it was actually Harry's idea," said Lulu.

"Thank you, Harry," said Mother, glancing around the kitchen, looking for him.

"You're most welcome, Mother," said Harry, bowing. But Mother had already turned to tend to Sam and did not appear to have heard or seen Harry.

While Mother was all smiles about her break, Sam was not. He looked with concern at the two women in his life. He frowned, blew a big spit bubble and looked to Harry for help.

Harry shrugged his many shoulders and said, "Sorry, young sir. It's out of my hands." Then Harry went into a spin, trying to catch up with his shrugging shoulders in order to stop them.

And that night, Sam ate an extra-huge supper, planning ahead for the worst the next morning.

CHAPTER TWO

Lulu got up with the first *cock-a-doodle-do* from the rooster who resided at Farmer Wallenhaupt's farm.

"C'mon, sleepyhead." She nudged Harry.

Harry groaned and straightened his top hat, which had gone askew in his sleep. He rolled over and stared at his reflection in the glass top of Lulu's nightstand. "The sun's still in bed," he mumbled.

"Nonsense! There's sunshine all over the yard!" Lulu said. She pulled back the curtain and showed the bright outside world to her friend.

They went to the kitchen, still in their pajamas. Lulu opened the window as she had seen Mother do every summer morning since forever. Outside, green leaves rippled on the trees, and the air was fragrant with blossoms.

"This will be a snap," said Lulu.

"Oh, yes, surely." Harry nodded slowly.

"This will be *easy!*"

"I'm quite certain." But Harry did not look quite certain.

"So where do we begin?"

Harry looked at her. "Begin?"

"Yes. What do we do first?"

"Well, perhaps, er, ahem, what I mean to say is . . . if you're going to feed *Sam,* perhaps you should actually have *Sam* at hand."

"Of course!" said Lulu. "Thanks, Harry, old buddy. You always know what to do. That's why I keep you around."

"Indeed," said Harry. "I am the answer man."

They went off to get Sam.

"Sam," Lulu whispered, hanging over the crib.

"Wake up, young sir," Harry said softly.

Sam did not stir.

"Up 'n' at 'em!" Lulu said, more loudly this time.

"Rise and shine!" Harry added.

Sam woke up and smiled grandly. Then he realized that this was the morning Lulu was to make his breakfast.

Lulu swept him up from his crib and placed him on the floor. "Follow me, mister," she said.

Please understand, Sam was no ordinary toddler. He was a kid on the ball; a kid who knew which end was up; a kid who figured that a breakfast made by Lulu Atlantis would not be quite the dish Mother would serve him. He followed his sister warily, looking about desperately for Mother.

When Lulu lifted Sam up into his chair, he moaned.

Sam watched his sister. His worried eyes showed that he did not have much hope.

"Well now, first . . . ," Lulu said tentatively, not knowing quite how to go about this.

"A bowl, perhaps, miss?" Harry suggested.

"Just the thing, sir!" Lulu pulled down Sam's breakfast bowl, the one with fire engines that lit up when you put water in it.

"And next . . . ," said Lulu, tentatively once again.

"Oatmeal, miss?" suggested Harry.

"Oatmeal it is, sir!" Lulu grinned and winked.

Sam frowned.

Lulu brought the round oatmeal box down from the cupboard.

"And . . . ?"

"Water?" Harry suggested. "Milk?" he suggested.

"Absolutely, O Most Intelligent One!" said Lulu, grinning and bowing to Harry. (Harry bowed back.)

Lulu mixed together the oatmeal and the water and the milk into a lumpy gray paste, just as she had seen Mother do every morning. She put the oatmeal into the microwave for two and a half minutes, just as Mother did. When the microwave beeped, she pulled the bowl out, placed it back on the counter and shook in some cinnamon and some nutmeg. Just like Mother.

Then she plunked the bowl down on the tray of Sam's high chair. Its fire engine lights twinkled merrily on and off.

"There you go, baby brother," she said. Her face beamed with pride at her accomplishment. She had made oatmeal, just like Mother!

Sam looked at the oatmeal and spun his head away. In fact, he turned his head so far and so fast, his entire body twisted and he arched himself away from his high-chair tray. He held up his arm, as if to shield his face from his breakfast.

"Yuck!" screamed Sam.

"What's the matter?" asked Lulu. "You didn't even taste it! Taste it! You'll love it!" She piled a spoon high with oatmeal and aimed it at Sam's mouth.

Sam shut his mouth tight. He tried to push the spoon away with his hands, but Lulu was stronger. She pried at his lips with the spoon. Sam scrunched his lips into a tight ball. He clamped both his hands over his mouth and squealed, "Nnnnnnnnnnnn!"

"Come *on*, Sam!" Lulu hissed through clenched teeth. She tried to pry his fingers away from his mouth. Unable to do so, she forced the spoon between them. Gray, mushy oatmeal oozed from the spoon, slithering down Sam's chin. It ran in slimy clumps onto his shirt and then onto his tray, a thick, gray river of oatmeal. Now Sam waved his fists frantically in the air, crashing his bowl onto the floor. The lights of the fire engine blinked on and off furiously. He spat the oatmeal into the air and flung the oatmeal all over his shirt and tray. It flew and stuck on the walls, the ceiling, the floor and Lulu's head.

"Hey!" shouted Lulu.

"NO!" shouted Sam.

Harry said nothing. He crouched bug-eyed, watching the spectacle.

"What now?" Lulu asked Harry.

"Maybe you need to add something to make it more palatable," Harry suggested.

"Like what?" said Lulu.

"What does Mother add? I've seen her add something," said Harry.

"What?" said Lulu.

"A secret ingredient," said Harry.

"Sugar?"

Harry shook his head.

"Cocoa?"

Harry shrugged and pursed his lips.

Sam started to whine. "Hungry," he said, sniffling.

"The eyes of pigeons? The wings of bats? The tongues of toads?" spat Lulu.

Harry scuttled across the counter and up the wall to the cupboard. He studied all the tins and jars Mother had stashed away. Sam said, "Hungry!" again, this time more loudly.

"Hmmmm. If I were a secret ingredient, where would I be?" Harry said over the sound of Sam's moaning and sniffling. "Help me find it, miss!" he demanded.

"Don't order me around, Harry," said Lulu.

"But your brother . . ."

"The heck with my brother! I'm *finished* here!" said Lulu. She flounced herself across the kitchen and stomped toward the door into the living room.

"Well, I'm going out. And I'm not coming back until I find that secret ingredient!" said Harry. He skittered over to the back door.

"Well, then . . . good . . . *bye!*" yelled Lulu over her shoulder.

CHAPTER THREE

Sam sat in the kitchen sulking. Lulu sulked in the living room. And Harry ran down the lane, looking for the secret ingredient.

Slumped on the couch, Lulu listened to Sam's sniffles in the kitchen, and to the silence coming from Mother's bedroom.

"Pssssst," she heard. She looked up. Yogurt Skunk stuck his head through the open living room window.

"What do *you* want?" snapped Lulu.

"Is that the way you talk to *all* your good buddies?" asked Yogurt Skunk.

"Yes! What do you want?" she snapped once more.

"It's what *you* might want, girlie," said Skunk. He didn't appear to care too much for Lulu's attitude this morning.

"And what might that be?"

"You might want to rescue your old pal Harry, is what *that* might be," said Skunk.

Lulu jumped up. "Harry! Where is he?"

"He's presently in a turmoil, toots. Down at Farmer Wallenhaupt's raspberry patch. And that's all I'm gonna say till you sweeten up, sugar." With that, Yogurt Skunk disappeared from the window.

Lulu ran through the kitchen and out the door. As the door swung shut behind her, she heard a yelp.

"Sam!" Lulu said out loud, slapping her forehead with the palm of her hand.

Sam was still in his high chair all alone in the kitchen, rolling his eyes and banging his hands on his tray. "Hungry, hungry, hungry," he babbled.

Lulu ran out to the garden, found Yogurt Skunk behind a clump of phlox, yanked him by the tail and said, "Watch Sam!" She pushed him in the direction of the kitchen and then she took off, out of the garden and down Sweet Pea Lane toward Farmer Wallenhaupt's raspberry patch.

Lulu tore so quickly down the lane, dust kicked up behind her in clouds. Her legs spun like bicycle wheels all the way to the raspberry patch. When she got there, she slid into such a sharp turn, she skidded, fell and skinned her knees. Jumping right up, she ran to the fence surrounding the patch.

"Harry!" she called.

She heard nothing in response, save for an odd, soft hissing sound.

"HARRY!"

And then she heard it. A tiny, tiny . . . "Miss?" whispered in a tiny, tiny voice.

Sensing trouble, Lulu Atlantis took a deep breath and ventured in.

CHAPTER FOUR

"Harry?" Lulu whispered.

Nothing.

And then . . . *hiiiissssssssssss!*

Snakes. The raspberry patch was slithering with

snakes. Their luminescent scales shone in the dewy sunlight and their tails curled in rapture at the very taste of the berries.

"*Sssssweeet,*" Lulu heard them hiss. "*Ssssssensssa-tional,*" they hissed some more. "*Exccccccccccccellent!*"

Lulu spotted Harry. He hung suspended over the ground, gripping a raspberry high up on a raspberry bush for dear life. Below him, coiled tightly, was a snake the color of shadows. The snake's tongue darted in and out of his mouth. His head waved back and forth, back and forth, as he got ready to strike.

The other snakes, though not hearing (since they had no ears), knew that both Lulu and Harry were there. Their bodies vibrated from the tread of Lulu's feet, and from the shiver of Harry's body.

All the snakes turned their heads to look first at Harry, and then at Lulu. They dropped their raspberries from their opened jaws and darted their forked tongues in and out of their mouths. They slithered their way over the ground, to gather around the snake who was getting ready to make breakfast of poor Harry.

The snakes squinted their eyes up to scare Lulu and Harry. They pulled their scaly bodies into tight coils, to show how fierce they were.

"Harry! Hold on!" whispered Lulu.

"Yes, miss. What else would I do?" Harry whispered back.

Please understand, the branches of the raspberry bushes of Farmer Wallenhaupt were so very heavy with luscious berries that the slightest movement caused berries to shake loose and tumble to the ground. Harry's whispers to Lulu were enough to cause the berry to which he clung to fall from its branch. Harry found himself plunging to the earth, straight toward the snakes! Quickly he grasped another berry and held on. His hands slid, then stopped. The snakes turned their heads toward the commotion.

Now was the time! With the backs of the snakes' heads to her, Lulu bent down and picked up several large shards of flint from the ground. She took aim and skimmed one through the air, directly over the snakes' heads, aiming for the bushes directly opposite Harry. The shard of flint did as Lulu had intended it to do. It crashed its way through the bushes and slammed against the fence behind them. It made a racket, causing the berries to shake and shiver, and the fence to vibrate.

Lulu threw the other pieces of stone, all in different directions, all away from Harry. They crashed against the fence in several places. The snakes slithered this way and that, craning their necks (which were actually their entire bodies), looking to see what made all the quaking and quivering in their raspberry patch. Was it Farmer Wallenhaupt coming with his axe? Was it his wicked wife, coming with her kitchen knife?

With the snakes preoccupied, Lulu jumped over their heads, landing on tiptoe near Harry's raspberry bush. She grabbed him by several of his hands, spun him through the air and pushed him into her hair, where he held on tight.

The snakes were still looking here and looking there, writhing their bodies in big question marks, hissing and checking under the raspberry bushes and behind the bushes and through the fence. They knocked into each other as they wriggled across the ground.

Lulu took a deep breath and held it. Harry took a deep breath as well, and shut his eyes tight. Lightly, lightly, Lulu tiptoed backward out of the raspberry patch, stepping carefully through the confused snakes. Only when she was all the way outside did she dare breathe.

Harry felt her breathe, and *he* breathed. He opened his eyes and stuck his head out of Lulu's hair. He and Lulu peered through the bushes and watched the snakes calm down and return to their raspberries. Apparently they had turned to matters other than the possibility of spiders and young girls for breakfast.

"How quickly they forget," said Harry.

"Holy Toledo!" said Lulu.

"Well, that didn't work out," said Harry.

"No, Harry, it certainly did not."

"Are you still mad at me?"

"Would I be here if I were?" replied Lulu.

Harry smiled, straightened his bow tie and tilted his hat to a roguish angle. "So now what? We've got no secret ingredient. And Sam's hungry."

"Well, I guess Sam'll just have to starve," snapped Lulu.

"Where is he, anyway?" asked Harry.

"In his high chair."

"*Alone?*"

"Nope. Yogurt Skunk's babysitting," said Lulu.

Harry rolled his eyes to the sky. "Holy Toledo," he whispered, as he skittered down Lulu's arm, spun a quick rope of his spider silk, and let himself gently onto the floor.

When the two friends got to the kitchen, they found Yogurt Skunk draped around Sam's shoulders. The skunk was tickling Sam's ear with his soft, moist nose. Sam was giggling.

Harry was relieved.

"What? You think I don't know how to babysit? How hard is it to sit a baby?" asked Skunk, seeing the look on Harry's face.

"Well . . . ," Harry said.

"You think I don't know what I'm doin'? You think I never sat a baby before? Well, maybe you're right," said Yogurt Skunk in a sarcastic tone of voice. He slinked down from Sam's shoulders and made his way across the floor to Harry. He puffed up his fur, looking bigger and bolder and scarier the closer he got. "Maybe I *don't* know how to sit a baby, 'cause I'm too busy spendin' my time eating click beetles. And lizards. And *top-hatted spiders*! Top-hatted spiders are *always* first on my lunch menu!"

Harry made a mad dash up Lulu's side and back into her snarled hair.

Yogurt Skunk grinned, then looked up at Lulu. "Why so glum, chum?" he asked.

"Sam won't eat my oatmeal. Harry and me, we're trying to think of the secret ingredient Mother adds, so Sam will eat."

"Let the kid go hungry," said Skunk, shrugging.

"I can't let my brother go hungry. Besides, he'll moan and whine and cry and drive us all crazy!" said Lulu.

"Welp, you got a problem there," said Skunk. "My question is . . . whyn't you ask me first of all? What you need, kiddo, is the Gangsters' Bakery. They'll figure out your secret ingredient for you, that's for darn tootin'."

Skunk told them exactly what route to take to get to the Gangsters' Bakery quickly.

"You keep babysitting, then," said Lulu.

"No sweat, pet," said Skunk. He called after Lulu and Harry, "Just tell 'em the Skunk sent you! Oh, and might I suggest you change out of them *pajamas?*"

On their merry way, Harry (who was not so merry) said, "Are you sure you want to take the advice of a *skunk?*"

"Oh, hush, Harry," said Lulu, and poked him back down into her pocket.

CHAPTER FIVE

The Gangsters' Bakery was down a leafy lane, over a battered bridge and through an alleyway that appeared out of nowhere. This being the country, the alleyway came as a bit of a shock. Who expected alleyways in the middle of a country lane?

The door of the bakery was the color of mud, pitted and dirty and looking as if many a foot had kicked at it. And there appeared to be bullet holes in it too!

Lulu knocked timidly. Immediately, a tiny window opened at the top of the door and Lulu saw flinty eyes squinting down at her.

"Wwwwarrruuuwaannnnnd?" rumbled a gnarly voice.

Her heart hammering, Lulu said exactly what Skunk

had told her to say. "The Skunk sent us." Her little voice shook like a dry leaf in a winter wind.

The tiny window slammed shut and the heavy door creaked open.

Before them was a vast, shiny white-tiled kitchen filled to the ceiling with bangs, clangs, clatters, platters, glistening steel bowls, whirring blenders, sacks of sugar, bags of flour, bins of raisins, barrels of icing, batches of cookie dough, bundles of chocolate chips, bottles of sprinkles, pitchers of cream, kettles of syrup and huge, warm ovens.

Lulu stood on the threshold and Harry stood on Lulu's shoulder. They looked across the bakery kitchen to where two men with glowers on their sour faces stood behind a long marble counter. One man held a large steel spoon, and the other held a silver wire whisk. They were stirring and whipping up a storm. The third man, the one who had let Lulu and Harry in, stalked over to the counter and stood like a hulk beside the other two. He picked up an electric hand mixer. The three of them stirred and whipped and whirred and scowled at Lulu and Harry. The men gnashed their teeth as if they were hungry wolves.

Lulu and Harry gawked.

The man at the end of the counter was as thin as a wire. He had a huge, beaked nose and a very long neck on which his narrow head bobbed back and forth. He wore a black shirt, a black tie and a black fedora, all splattered with spatters of icing in blue, in green and in pink, and with cake batter in vanilla. An official brass name tag was pinned to his shirt. The badge had a blob of pink icing on it. Black letters on the badge said:

GANGSTER BAKER
Scarecrow

He was the man holding the large steel spoon.

The man next to him was short and pale and very neat-looking, with no spatters or splatters. This man was crisp and so clean he sparkled! He wore a blue shirt with pink polka dots and a matching bow tie, both of which were starched to within an inch of their lives. The baker's hat that stood tall on his head was as white as white could be. On it was an official name tag just like the one on Baker Scarecrow. This badge said:

GANGSTER BAKER
Lefty-Righty Louie

He was the man holding the silver wire whisk.

The third man, the one who had let them in the door, was greatly round and had a red face. He wore a dingy white chef's jacket with a thick leather belt around his middle. The ends of the belt barely met over his belly. On his jacket was yet another official name tag that read:

GANGSTER PASTRY CHEF

Jimmy Creamcheese

He set the electric mixer down, cracked his knuckles mightily, glared at Lulu, then picked his mixer back up and started mixing again.

Lulu, with Harry hanging on tight to her shoulder, tiptoed timidly toward the men. She had her hands deep in her pockets, squeezing the good-luck stones Yogurt Skunk had given her.

With extreme trepidation, she and Harry drew up to the counter.

"Keep your eyes on those guys," whispered Harry.

Lulu nodded. She barely heard Harry's whisper over the thud of her heartbeat resounding in her ears.

The three men stopped stirring and whipping and

mixing. They stood stock-still and stared at Lulu. The kitchen was suddenly shrouded in a thick and frosty silence.

"S'posed ta be here, are you?" Baker Scarecrow squawked.

Lulu jumped, startled by the loud, shrill voice.

"Y-yes . . . ?" piped Lulu in a tiny voice. Her heart beat so hard against her chest, she thought it was going to break clear through.

"Pssst!" whispered Harry. "Yes, *sir*, miss! Be polite!"

Lulu didn't have a chance to be polite. Gangster Pastry Chef Jimmy Creamcheese rasped in his low, scratchy voice, "She says da Skunk sent her. Youse guys t'ink da Skunk sent her?" he asked his fellow bakers.

"I wouldn't know," said Baker Lefty-Righty Louie.

Baker Scarecrow shrugged his skinny shoulders, jabbing them up and down, up and down.

Jimmy Creamcheese's red face grew redder and redder. His rotund belly looked as if it would pop the buttons off his jacket.

Lulu shook like Jell-O. Harry almost fainted on her shoulder.

Then Baker Lefty-Righty Louie frowned down at Lulu and tsked. He reached over the counter with his wire whisk and tapped Lulu nimbly on the head with it. It hurt and Lulu rubbed the top of her head.

"Who are you?" he demanded in a voice as sharp as a knife blade.

"I'm L-Lulu Atlantis from S-S-Sweet P-Pea Lane," stuttered Lulu.

He tapped her on the head once again, one tap per word, saying, "What (tap) do (tap) you (tap) want (tap)?"

Lulu and Harry gulped and shivered in their shoes and hugged each other.

"Awwk!" Baker Scarecrow screeched, leaning over

the counter toward Lulu, tilting his head and peering at the frightened look on her face. "*Skeered?* What're we, ugly?"

Chef Jimmy Creamcheese grumbled, "Yeah, gotch-yerself a problem, girlie? Whacha starin' at?"

And Baker Lefty-Righty Louie spat, "You're not so pretty yourself, my dear!"

Lulu tried to speak, but her voice was nowhere to be found.

Harry rose to the occasion. He cleared his throat: "Emmm-hemmmm . . ."

The gangsters quieted down and scrutinized the area from which came Harry's "Emmm-hemmmm."

"Who said dat?" asked Jimmy Creamcheese.

Scarecrow turned his head first to the left and then to the right. He inspected Lulu with one eye.

"There! On the girl's shoulder," said Lefty-Righty Louie.

"Dat's a *bug!*" cried Jimmy Creamcheese, crunching up his fat nose. *"I hate bugs!"*

Quickly, Harry said, "No, no. Not a bug. A *spider*, to be exact." He grinned a nervous grin that was far too large for his little face. He continued, "Oh, kind sirs, we have no problem with *youse* guys at all! On the contrary, we admire *youse* guys! You are lovely and so is your lovely kitchen. All lovely. Heh, heh. Um. Uh. Well. Um. Well. The point *is*—Skunk told us you might help us."

"Somebody botherin' ya, girlie? Ya want I should take care o' him?" boomed Jimmy Creamcheese. "I could rub him out in a second."

"Oh, no! No rubbing out, thank you . . . *youse* . . . kindly just the same. *Please* no rubbing out!" Harry squeaked.

Lulu took a deep breath and stood tall. She held her head high and said, in a voice as shrill as a piccolo,

"We've come to see if you can bake us the Secret Ingredient."

"Ya mean dis is a *bakery* visit, not a *gangster* visit," rumbled Chef Jimmy.

"Correct, sir," said Harry, wiping perspiration from his brow.

"*Yes*, sir," whispered Lulu, wiping perspiration from *her* brow.

"Secret Ingredient? Ahhhwwk! Come to the right place, you have! The right place!" said Scarecrow.

"Absolutely!" said Lefty-Righty Louie, straightening his baker's hat with the end of his whisk. "We've got the goods for goodies, all right! And here's the proof of the pudding." He handed Lulu a cookie, and to Harry he handed a crumb just big enough to suit him.

Lulu cautiously took her cookie and Harry cautiously took his crumb. They held their treats in front of their faces, too scared to take a bite.

"Eat dat cookie, girlie!" ordered Chef Jimmy.

It was large, round, golden and still warm from the oven. On it were chocolate and rainbow sprinkles, dusted with a snowfall of powdery sugar. It was edged with pink icing, formed in a circle of roses.

Lulu bit into her cookie. Harry bit into his crumb.

Lulu's eyes closed. "MMMMMMMMMMMMMMM!"

"The Perfect Cookie!" Harry crooned.

"MMMMMMMMMMMM!" Lulu said once again.

The gangsters let Lulu and Harry finish their cookies. Then Chef Jimmy demanded, "So what's dis secret ingredient youse guys want?"

"Sam," Lulu said.

"Sam! Sam? Never baked no *sam!*" Scarecrow squawked once more.

Lulu shivered. She whispered, "My little brother. That's what Sam is." And then she added, a bit more strongly and with a sharp, almost brave, bob of her head, "And he needs breakfast."

"So go home 'n' feed 'im!" shouted Chef Jimmy. He burst into a horrid laugh. The others laughed with him. Lulu trembled. She and Harry gripped each other until it hurt.

"Dere's gotta be more ta tell dan dat. What's da *real* story?" said Jimmy Creamcheese. "C'mon, spit it out. We ain't got all day." And he picked up his electric hand mixer, bent way over the counter and pointed the mixer right at Lulu's nose.

CHAPTER SIX

Taking a deep breath, Lulu squeezed the stones in her pocket and said, "The real story? I'll tell you the real story!" And this is what she said:

"Mother is getting on in years."

Chef Jimmy slowly lowered his mixer. "I got a elderly ma, too," he murmured. He blew his nose violently into a dirty dishcloth.

Lulu continued, "Father's never home."

"My father was never home either," said Lefty-Righty Louie, his voice quivering. "Never *ever!*" He dropped his wire whisk, picked up a clean dish towel with both hands and covered his mouth with it.

"Sam hogs *all* Mother's attention and I feel invisible!" said Lulu.

"Noooo-bod-y notices me neeee-either!" yawped Scarecrow. "Even when I want 'em to!" He dabbed at his eyes with his sleeve, smearing colorful globs of icing and cake batter all over his face.

"I tried running away, but that didn't work, so now I live in a house where everybody *just ignores me!*" Lulu was on a roll.

"I know what it's like not to fit in," sighed Lefty-Righty Louie, shaking his head forlornly.

"*And* I got stuck in the Umbrella Tree with a killer spider and then I tried to save Harry and got stuck in a raspberry patch with killer snakes!"

At that, each one of the gangsters truly burst into tears, sobbing. They ran out from behind the counter and clustered around Lulu.

"Poor liddle tyke-a-roonie," they cried, wiping their faces and blowing their noses into dish towels.

Lulu looked at Harry and Harry looked at Lulu. Neither of them knew what to make of gangsters who a moment ago had been fierce, frightening fiends and were now dissolved in tears!

"So dis secret ingredient? What's dat fer?" asked Chef Jimmy, sniffling and gaining some control of his emotions.

"I promised Mother I'd feed Sam his breakfast today. I made him oatmeal and he threw it on the floor and spat it on the wall and it even got on my face and in my hair. See?" and Lulu held out a strand of her hair, stiff and gummy with old oatmeal. "I need to make him a breakfast he'll eat, to help Mother out," she explained.

"Of course you do, liddle one. You simply *must* help your elderly mama out," piped Lefty-Righty Louie. He dabbed gently at his teary eyes with a new dish towel, as white as his baker's hat.

Jimmy Creamcheese grunted and Scarecrow jumped excitedly from one foot to the other. He rubbed at his face with his arm. By this time, his face was entirely covered in colorful icing and looked like the inside of a kaleidoscope.

"The Skunk told us you could give us a secret ingredient to make Sam eat," said Lulu. She held her hands together, fingers interlocked, in a pleading manner. "Can you do it? Can you give us a secret ingredient to make Sam eat?" she begged.

"*Dat's* all? Oh, sister, can *we* help *you!* Hop to it, ya mugs!" cried Chef Jimmy.

And with that, the gangsters patted Lulu on the back and on the head and on the shoulder, turned as one and leaped back behind their counter. They pulled out boxes and jars. They poured! They whipped! They stirred and blended and beat! They smiled and hummed rough melodies.

When they were finished stirring and blending and beating, they each poured their separate batters into one baking tin. Gently, they slid the tin into an oven already warm. The kitchen filled with an aroma that would make an angel cry, if the aroma made it all the way up to heaven. Lulu and Harry glanced up at the ceiling, waiting to see if angels would filter through.

When at last the gangsters were done, they lifted a spectacular, fabulous, gorgeous, exquisite, beautiful, fragrant golden bowl of something high into the air for all to see.

"What's that?" asked Lulu.

"Why, liddle tyke-a-roonie, I thoughtcha knew. Dat's da Secret Ingredient," said Chef Jimmy.

Lulu sniffed with her nose in the air. "AAAAahhh-hhhhh," she sighed. "It smells *wonderful!*"

"Tastes wonderful too. *Heavenly!*" said Lefty-Righty Louie, clasping his hands beneath his chin and sniffing in the aroma.

The gangsters stood, Scarecrow to the right of Chef Jimmy and Lefty-Righty Louie to the left. Jimmy Creamcheese held the golden bowl of Secret Ingredient out to Lulu, offering it to her. Lulu held out her hands shyly to receive it.

"Ummm, how much does it cost?" whispered Lulu, suddenly worried.

"Uh-oh," said Harry, knowing they had no money.

"Aw, shucks. Youse guys got enough problems on yer hands. Here. It's fer free," said Jimmy Creamcheese.

"Oh, thank you so much!" Lulu said, her smile glowing over the golden bowl in her hands.

"I'm going to make you all handsome, glamorous and stylish top hats, as a way of saying thanks!" said Harry.

"One for each of us?" Scarecrow actually warbled,

hardly believing his ears (which were presently spotted with pink cake batter and green frosting).

"Of course! I'll weave them of silver cobwebs, my
very finest," said Harry.

"Whoa. . . ." The gangsters grunted and growled and
shuffled their feet, not knowing how to handle happiness.

As she and Harry left, Lulu called good-bye to the
gangsters.

"Come back and visit, Lulu Atlantis from Sweet Pea
Lane!" cried Lefty-Righty Louie as they all waved and
sniffled. They dabbed at their eyes with dish towels
and wrapped their arms around each other's shoulders
in the emotion of the moment.

Lulu carried the Secret Ingredient close to her heart all
the way home. The bowl led the way with a golden
glow that lit the underside of Lulu's chin, just as a

buttercup will light the underside of your chin with the sunny color yellow.

Harry sat on Lulu's shoulder, keeping one eye on the bowl and the other eye on the road. He hoped they would not be accosted by highwaymen. He also hoped that at home, the skunk was not eating the baby, or doing anything else unpleasant.

When at last they arrived home, they heard Sam bawling his head off. The kitchen door was flung open and there stood Yogurt Skunk, completely frazzled. "IT'S ABOUT TIME! WHAT'S THE IDEA? WHY DIDN'T YOU GUYS TELL ME THESE THINGS CRY? YOUR MOTHER COULD SLEEP THROUGH A TOR-NADO!" he yelled.

Sam continued to cry, extending his arms to his sister. He wriggled his hands back and forth at her in desperation.

Skunk screamed on. "MY HEAD'S GONNA *EX-PLODE*! I'M . . . I'M . . . hey! (Skunk's tone changed completely—sniff sniff.) What's that? (Sniff.) Hey! Is that my pay for babysitting the little stinker?" Yogurt Skunk grabbed the bowl.

"How *nice* of you to think of me," he gushed.

Before Lulu could yell *STOP!*, Skunk upended the bowl, opened his mouth hugely and scarfed down the entire contents.

He licked his lips and his eyes rolled to heaven. "Mmmm-mmmmmmm! Thanks, toots! Don't call me; I'll call you!" he said, and was gone in the blink of an eye.

CHAPTER SEVEN

Lulu stood in Mother's kitchen, sagging in complete defeat. Harry sagged at her side. And Sam cried.

Mother came into the kitchen from her bedroom. She yawned and rubbed her eyes. Her hair was mussy with nighttime but still had rivers of light flowing through it. She smiled.

"What's all the racket?" she said.

Lulu looked at the floor.

"Did Sam eat?" Mother asked.

Sam bawled even more loudly in response. Lulu continued to look at the floor. So did Harry.

Mother said, "I see that the oatmeal box is on the counter, and Sam's bowl is on the floor."

"Yes. He wouldn't eat his breakfast," whispered Lulu.

"Why not?" asked Mother. "Why not, dear?" she said, moving close to Lulu.

"He hated the oatmeal I made. I couldn't figure out the secret ingredient," said Lulu.

"Oh! I always thought you knew, Lulu Atlantis," said Mother, caressing Lulu's chin with soft fingers. "Watch."

Mother went over to the counter, pulling the sash

of her robe tighter. She smiled and hummed and poured oatmeal flakes into another of Sam's bowls. This one was blue with white polka dots. She poured some water into the bowl. She put the bowl in the microwave and cooked it on high for two and one half minutes. She sang a lively tune and did a pirouette to help pass the time. She curtsied to Sam, who was no longer crying and looked, for the first time, hopeful.

Mother took the bowl out, put it on the counter and stirred. Then she reached for the cinnamon and shook a bit over the bowl. Then she reached for the nutmeg, stuck her index finger and her thumb into the jar, and added exactly one pinch of nutmeg to the oatmeal.

"And now for the Secret Ingredient," she said. She picked up the bowl and held it so that Lulu and Harry could see.

Then Mother took the fingers of her hand and held them to her lips. She kissed a sweet kiss onto her fingers, held them over the bowl and blew the kiss into the oatmeal.

"My Secret Ingredient," said Mother, and placed the bowl gently on Sam's high-chair tray.

Next morning, as Harry sat above the corner cupboard spinning gangsters' hats out of his finest silver cobwebs, Lulu prepared Sam's breakfast all by herself. She and Harry fed him. And Sam gobbled it all down, every last bite.

Later, Mother made blueberry pancakes and bacon for Lulu. With a Secret Ingredient mixed in, of course.

part three
The Season of Monsters

CHAPTER ONE

It all happened in the snowy winter when Sam was still a toddler, albeit a bigger toddler by this time.

It all happened just a few days after Lulu had sent Yogurt Skunk packing.

Yogurt Skunk had gotten into the garbage can on

Lulu's back porch. Since his kitchen garden was covered in ice and snow, he'd had to forage for food in other places. Lulu had dragged a broom onto the back porch, where Skunk had tossed toast crusts and eggshells and rotten lettuce leaves and coffee grounds and half-eaten apples.

"Get out of here!" Lulu had yelled.

"Aaaw, have a heart, Lulu. Winter's hard on skunks. I'm hungry!"

"You made a huge mess, and *I* have to clean it up!" Lulu said.

"Let Mother clean it up," suggested Skunk. He shrugged his shoulders and held out his hands, palms up, at the simplicity of his solution.

"*Mother* is too *busy* chasing the *toddler*! I'm the slave around here. Now scram!"

With freezing fingers, Lulu pushed the broom against the garbage, at the same time managing to sideswipe Skunk with it. He fell over sideways.

"Yow!" said Skunk.

"Too bad," said Lulu.

"Look, I can help you clean up," offered Yogurt Skunk. He grabbed the broom from Lulu's hands and twirled it around . . . right through Mother's kitchen window. The glass crashed into a thousand twinkling slivers.

Lulu grabbed the broom back and took a swing at him. "Now we're in for it!" she yelled.

"But . . . but . . . I was just trying to help," Skunk said.

"Beat it!"

Skunk tried again. "Hey, listen. We're buddies, right? Heh, heh. Pals helping each other? Ya know, toots?"

"Don't call me toots! I'm not *pals* with you OR ANYBODY ELSE!" Lulu yelled. She swung the broom at Skunk again, this time clobbering his head.

"Hey! Ouch!"

"SCRAM!" Lulu kicked at him, missing him by barely an inch.

And Skunk did scram, sniffling and rubbing his head. Tears ran down his furry cheeks. With that one shoo of Lulu's broom, Yogurt Skunk disappeared from the face of the earth. The last thing Lulu heard from him was this, spoken through tears: "Some way to treat a friend."

"Good riddance," said Lulu, now in Quite the Mood.

Lulu swept up the garbage, leaving some of it in the corners of the porch but getting most of it back into the garbage can. She stomped inside, slamming the door behind her.

"That's not like you, Miss Lulu Atlantis. True friends are hard to come by," said Harry, who sat in his web. The web was fixed to the corner of the window in the kitchen door, where Harry could see everything that happened on the porch. Spiders, being of a delicate nature, do not venture out much in winter. They are therefore in need of good vantage points throughout their houses from which to keep an eye on things inside and out.

"Too bad," said Lulu. "Besides, I don't need friends. What I need is *True Blue Love.*"

"What do you think True Blue Love is, miss?" said Harry, shaking his head. "A love that is True Blue is *friendship.* Friendship that is deep and trustworthy and—"

"And *blah, blah, blah!*" Lulu rudely interrupted. "Words! I'm sick of them! *Show me! Find me some True Blue Love!*"

Harry said, "Well, miss, it seems to me that to find True Blue Love, you would not have to search beyond your own backyard."

"Oh, right. Su-u-ure." Lulu sank into a kitchen chair and chewed her thumb. She shivered in the thin finger of cold wind blowing through the broken window. She frowned.

Harry climbed onto the tabletop, a serious expression clouding his bright eyes. He crouched in front of Lulu. "What are you thinking, miss?"

"I'm thinking I'm going to be in trouble with Mother," Lulu said. "Stupid Yogurt Skunk!" she added as an afterthought.

"Is there anything *else* bothering you?"

Lulu sighed. She hung her head and let the finger of wind blow her hair into her eyes. "I'm thinking about Father, Harry. Father knows about True Blue Love. He could tell me where I could find it. I know he could. It's in all his stories. I love Father's stories."

"We all love Father's stories," Harry said.

"Why does he always have to go away all the time?"

"Father is a crusader by nature. Haven't you always said he's your knight in shining armor? Knights in shining armor go on crusades."

"Knights in shining armor stay at *home*, protecting their damsels in distress. *Me*, to be exact. Aren't *I* as important as the Flammulated Owl or the Ozark Big-Eared Bat? Aren't *I* as important as the Houston Toad? Why does he love owls and toads and *parrots* more than me? What am I . . . chopped liver?" cried Lulu, banging her hand on the table so hard, she caused Harry to tumble over backward. When he had righted himself and regained his equilibrium, he straightened his hat, cleared his throat and looked at Lulu.

"Chopped liver? Never! Miss Lulu, your father loves—"

"Don't say another word, Harry!"

"Just because your father leaves, it does not mean he doesn't love you."

"I only know that if Father were here, life would be easy and I'd have all the answers. I'd know all about

True Blue Love. This . . . is . . . very . . . *frustrating!*"
Lulu shot her words straight at Harry. Then she dropped her voice to a whisper and said, "And I miss him."

"Of *course* you—"

Lulu smacked both hands down flat on the table. "I *told* you not to say *another word!*"

"I'm only trying to say—" began Harry.

Lulu leaned over the table and blew. She blew hard at Harry, skimming him along the slippery tabletop.

Please understand, when a person blows at a spider, especially a spider as frail and light as a daddy longlegs, it is an insult. When a person blows at a spider who is usually the person's best friend, it is the greatest insult of all. One can insult a spider more only by squishing the spider with the sole of one's shoe!

Harry twirled and rolled and skated across the tabletop, around and around, losing his top hat in the process. When he finally came to a halt, he leaned over to retrieve his hat, looked back at his best friend, his own True Blue Love, and sighed. He placed his hat straight up on his head, turned and clambered down the table leg. When he found a dark corner, he sat in it, watching Lulu chew her thumb and mourn the loss of her father.

There is a lot to be said for Harry at this point. Another spider, a spider having a weak moral fiber or a shallow character, would have packed his bags and left town. He would have left Lulu in the lurch. But Harry was a spider of great moral fiber and a deep and strong character. He was not going to abandon her.

If truth be known, Harry was rather relieved during those days following the disappearance of Yogurt Skunk. For the first time since he and Lulu had met the skunk, Harry felt like he was not on the menu as someone's lunch.

Lulu felt neither happy nor relieved. After that snowy winter day on which she turned away two friends, she just kept sweeping away at life, pushing it far away, deep into dark corners.

It was but two days after Yogurt Skunk disappeared from the face of the earth when the monster of Lulu's own childhood returned and took up residence under Sam's crib. Please remember that—just *two* days.

CHAPTER TWO

Surely it was nothing more than a mere mouse. At least, that was the case according to Mother, who said, "It's nothing more than a mere mouse."

Lulu and Harry and Mother stood in Sam's nursery. Sam was sitting up in his crib. Mother pinched her lips together with her fingers. She tapped the toes of her right foot against the floor. Her foot was encased in a terry-cloth slipper, so her tapping had more of a soft *shumphing* sound.

Harry, who had forgiven Lulu for blowing at him, and Lulu, who had forgiven Harry for disagreeing about her father, stood close together. They tapped their toes. Sam tapped his fingers on his crib mattress.

All of them stared at Sam's crib—Mother, Lulu and Harry from the outside, Sam from the inside. They stared at the bars on the sides. They stared at the mattress and at the pillow and at Teddy the Bear.

Now Mother turned her eyes to the area beneath the crib, where the problem lurked. Lulu's and Harry's eyes followed Mother's, and together they stared. Sam leaned over the top edge of the crib wall, trying to peer down.

"A mere mouse, I tell you," said Mother.

Lulu looked at Harry.

Harry looked at Lulu.

Sam looked from Lulu to Harry to Mother. "Mousie?" he asked, his eyes full of doubt.

Lulu broke the silence. "But I *saw* it, Mother! It's *huge* and *hairy* and—"

"A mouse!" Mother insisted. "And that is that! Now I have to go fix things for Great-aunty and Grandpère's visit. Remember the Eggman, Lulu Atlantis," Mother said. "Remember to ask him in for hot chocolate, if he likes."

After Mother flounced out of Sam's nursery, Lulu said to Harry, "Mother seems stressed."

"The visit, you know," said Harry.

"Mother's aunty is enough to stress anybody."

"Not to mention her *grandpère*," Harry added.

"I'm glad they belong to her and not to us."

"Don't kid yourself, miss."

"Don' *kid*," advised Sam from his crib.

Lulu thought a moment and then said, changing the subject from Mother's relatives to mothers in general,

"Harry, there are just some things mothers don't understand. Monsters, for instance."

"I'm inclined to agree with you, miss," said Harry.

"Yike!" said Sam. Sam had taken to saying "Yike" often lately, seeing that the underneath of his crib was inhabited by a monster.

"Did you see the monster, Sam?" asked Lulu. She was worried. Who wants a monster living right down the hall? It's bad for the blood pressure. And as everyone knows about monsters, they may start in one room but before you know it, the entire house is overrun with them!

"Yike!" said Sam, and thudded his rear end down hard on the crib mattress. He slapped his hands up to the sides of his head, screwed his eyes up tight, stuck out his tongue and tore at his hair.

"Do you think he means 'yike' the *monster*, or 'yike' the visit?" asked Lulu.

"I'd say six of one, half a dozen of the other," said Harry.

They heard Mother banging pots and pans in the kitchen. They heard her shout, "The Eggman, Lulu Atlantis!"

"Well, what do you propose we do about the situation?" said Harry.

"Which one?" asked Lulu.

"The situation at hand, miss. The monster."

"Maybe the monster will get bored and go away, if he's left alone."

"Monsters do get bored easily. It's their limited intellectual capacity. Monsters are quite dull-witted, you know."

"Better not let him hear you say that."

"Oops," said Harry, covering his mouth with two of his hands. He looked worried. He peered underneath the crib, in the inhabited area, to see if he'd caused any trouble.

"Don't worry, Harry. It's the light of day. Nothing much happens with monsters in the light of day. It's the dark of night you have to worry about."

Sam sniffled and a tear ran down his cheek.

"Don't worry, Sam. We'll think of something," said Lulu. She patted his cheek. Still feeling in Quite the Mood, however, she ended up giving poor Sam a hard pinch.

"Ouch!" cried Sam.

"My, my," said Harry, glancing disapprovingly at Lulu.

Lulu ignored him. She turned and left the nursery to Sam and the monster. Harry rode out on her right big toe.

"Do you think someone should stand guard, miss?" said Harry.

"Nah," said Lulu.

Now, you know as well as I that a roomful of monsters is not the place in which to abandon a toddler.

Think of it! Think of all that a monster could do to a helpless little toddler! Why, the monster could scare him with scary faces, causing him to cry and to drool! The monster could pinch him! Nibble at his toes! Tickle him with feathers until he laughed so hard, he threw up! Why, a monster could throw him at the ceiling and hope he stuck! A monster could . . . could *eat him*! A fine kettle of fish for a toddler! Poor Sam.

CHAPTER THREE

While Sam sat helplessly in a state of danger in his own room, Lulu was dressing for her trip to the end of the driveway, to await the coming of the Eggman.

For as far back as Lulu could remember, the Eggman had been there to answer her hardest questions, questions even Harry had difficulty with. Questions such as "How do you measure the softness of feathers?" "What is the best way to count fireflies in a field?" "How do you tell if a baby chick has singing talent?"

Lulu put on her blue jeans inside out. She put on her red sweater inside out. She went out into the hall-way, to the closet by the front door. She took her yel-low winter coat off the hanger, turned *it* inside out, and put it on.

Harry caught her getting ready to go outside. "Lulu Atlantis, where are you going?"

"Mother needs eggs. I'm going to wait at the fence for the Eggman."

"But your clothes are all *inside out*! Or hadn't you noticed?" Harry straightened his bow tie and checked his reflection in the brass kickplate on the bottom of the door.

"You know it's good luck to wear stuff inside out," said Lulu.

"That is if you put it on inside out *accidentally*," Harry pointed out.

"So who's to know?" said Lulu. "You want to come with me?"

"Better not," said Harry. During the winter, Harry did not go outside with Lulu except upon the rare occasions on which he could be assured of suitable protection in a warm woolen mitten tucked inside a warm woolen pocket.

"Well, that's just dandy. All of a sudden I'm *all* out of friends! There's no True Blue Love for some of us, I see!" Lulu said as she stalked through the front door and slammed it behind her.

"See you," said Harry quietly to the closed door.

It was just after that, that a thud thudded and a clunk clunked from the vicinity of Sam's room. Sam cried, "Yike!"

"What was that?" Mother called from the kitchen.

"It was a thud and a clunk from the baby's room, Mother," Harry called back.

Mother didn't answer. Harry heard her walk

quickly into Sam's room and say, "Is my Sammy okay? Is that silly little mousie back?" And the door to Sam's room clicked shut.

The house became still. Harry remained in the hallway, waiting silently in the silent house.

About the Eggman, please understand that he was not your ordinary seller of eggs. He did not simply wait at the counter in the store for you to come in and ask, "May I have a dozen medium brown eggs, please?"

The Eggman had eyes the color of the brightest sky and hair the color of the sunniest sun. He wore a big smile and a checkered shirt with rolled-up sleeves. He had little pieces of hay sticking out of his hair (except when he combed it on Sundays) and grizzly whiskers on his cheeks and chin (except when he shaved them, also on Sundays).

The Eggman worked with Farmer Wallenhaupt

down the road. Early every morning when the mists lay low over the grass and the sun peeked out from above the jagged line of Black Mountain, the Eggman jogged down to the henhouse. He gathered eggs from the hens, clucking at them and assuring them that they had done a mighty fine job of laying.

The Eggman put the eggs in a cardboard box and set the box on the roof of his rusty green jalopy. He drove his jalopy all around the country roads, selling eggs to nearby farms and houses. He steered the steering wheel with his right hand. He held his left arm out the car window, clutching the cardboard box that rested on the roof. The Eggman sang out, "Eggs! Buy your eggs from the Eggman! Buy your eggs from me!" He was a man who loved his job.

Back at the end of the driveway, Lulu stamped her feet on the ground to keep warm. She could not shove her hands down in her pockets, since her coat was on inside out. She clenched her hands into fists within her mittens.

"Eggs! Buy your eggs from the Eggman!" Lulu heard the Eggman's song. The green jalopy rolled down the lane.

Lulu raised her hand, hailing the Eggman.

"Lulu Atlantis!" called the Eggman, pulling his jalopy up close to her. "Have any more stories for me today? Found any more Yogurt Skunks recently? Any more Frog Princes?"

"We think the monster's come back, and this time he's under Sam's crib," Lulu said.

"Uh-oh. Well, little lady, if anybody knows how to handle a monster, it's you! If there's a fight between Lulu Atlantis and some monster, *any* monster, I'll wager a bet on Lulu Atlantis any day!" said the Eggman cheerfully. "So what can I do you for today?"

"Mother wants one dozen medium browns," she said. "Please," she added, deciding to be polite despite the fact that the Eggman did not appear to take the return of the monster very seriously.

"My large whites are swell this morning," the Eggman suggested hopefully. He had far too many large whites and had to sell them. People favored his medium browns these days.

"Mother said medium browns, please," said Lulu.

"Mother knows what's good," said the Eggman.

Lulu handed him the money in exchange for the long carton of eggs he handed to her.

"Thank you!" said the Eggman.

When Lulu said nothing in return, he looked long and hard at her face.

"Everything all right?" asked the Eggman.

"Hunky-dory," said Lulu.

"Then why do you look so sad?" he persisted.

"I don't look sad," said Lulu, looking down at the

ground, not daring to look up into the Eggman's kind eyes.

The Eggman threw the money Lulu had given him into the jalopy's ashtray, which he used for a change holder, as he did not smoke. He reached out of his car and opened the carton of eggs in Lulu's hand.

"Lovely, huh?" said the Eggman cheerfully, changing the subject.

Lulu stared down at the eggs, their bald heads perched in two neat rows, like the heads of defeathered hens nestled in their boxes in the henhouse.

"Well . . ." Lulu hesitated, wondering about the loveliness of eggs. "They're just eggs." She shrugged.

"*Just* eggs!" the Eggman repeated, aghast at her words. "Why, Lulu Atlantis, I don't think you're yourself today. An egg is *not* just an egg. Here, hold out your hand."

Lulu did so. He placed a medium brown in the palm of her hand.

"Doesn't it fit nice? Just so," said the Eggman.

Lulu nodded, looking at the egg.

"Grand for carrying with you through life, as it's such a nice fit, isn't it?"

Lulu smiled. "Indeed," she said. She thought that was what Harry might have said, had he been there.

"Look how smooth the eggs are. A perfectly smooth oval," said the Eggman. "And inside . . ." The Eggman paused, looking at Lulu.

"What's inside?" asked Lulu.

"You tell me," said the Eggman.

"A yolk," said Lulu.

"Maybe. Or maybe a *double* yolk! Or *maybe*—a little yellow chick! Or *maybe*—a baby dinosaur! Hah! You *never* know what you got inside till you break open the shell!" The Eggman paused and leaned his face close to Lulu's face. His voice dropped to a whisper. "Once, I found the diamond dewdrop crown of a fairy princess inside a medium white!"

"Did not!" said Lulu.

"Did so! An egg, Lulu Atlantis, is an every-day surprise!"

"I've never looked at an egg that way," said Lulu, her voice lifting a bit in hope.

"Yessirree. A simple old egg is . . . not so simple!" said the Eggman. "You could keep an egg nearby for comfort," he added.

"I don't need comfort," said Lulu.

"Well, then, for a surprise," said the Eggman.

"My life has enough surprises, thank you," said Lulu.

"Well, then, just to make you feel fine."

"I feel fine," said Lulu. "Fine and dandy!" she spat.

"Lulu Atlantis, what is going on? You are *not* fine and dandy today, so don't tell me you are. You always tell me your problems! Why, how did I find out about the monster under your bed when you were a kid?"

"I guess I told you," said Lulu, in a small voice.

"And who introduced me to Harry? To Yogurt Skunk?" asked the Eggman.

"Me," said Lulu, in a smaller voice.

"And who cries on my shoulder every time her father goes away? Who cries on my shoulder till it gets waterlogged and looks like a piece of driftwood?" asked the Eggman.

Lulu sighed.

"So I think I know you well enough. And I would say that it looks to me like something's bothering you. What is it, Lulu?"

"Do you believe in True Blue Love, Mr. Eggman?" said Lulu.

The Eggman smiled. "Sure do!"

"What is it?"

"What is it? Well, hmmmm. That is certainly a good question," said the Eggman, rubbing his chin.

"Yes, what is it?" Lulu repeated her question.

"Let me see. True Blue Love. Is it an animal?"

"No," said Lulu.

"That was a rhetorical question. Don't need an answer. Bear with me. I'm thinking," said the Eggman.

"I'll bear with you," said Lulu.

"Let me start again. Is it an animal?" Here he stopped and looked at Lulu, but Lulu made a zipper motion with her hand and zipped her lips. The Eggman continued, "Is it a vegetable?" Again he looked at Lulu. Lulu remained silent but frowned deeply. "Well, then, is it a mineral?" he cried.

"No way!" said Lulu.

"Rhetorical," said the Eggman.

"Rhetorical," agreed Lulu.

"So, the question is: 'What is True Blue Love?' Well, little lady, that is a hard one. Can I think on it?" the Eggman asked.

"I guess so." Lulu shrugged. "Anyway, Mother says would you like to come in for your hot chocolate today?"

"No time today. I got too many large whites to sell.

You tell Mother thank you kindly anyways." The Eggman smiled and drove slowly off in his huffing, puffing jalopy.

Lulu covered the medium brown gently with her fingers and it remained close-fitted in the palm of her hand. The carton of its brothers was in her other hand. And when she got home, both Mother and Harry were waiting for her at the door.

CHAPTER FOUR

Mother smiled, taking the eggs from Lulu. She opened the carton, took out several, and cracked them in fine lines across their middles.

Lulu watched the yolks within the egg whites, yellow as suns glowing on snow, slide gracefully into the mixing bowl. "Let me know if you find any dinosaurs or tiny crowns," she said.

"What are you talking about?" asked Mother.

"Nothing." Lulu held her chin in her hands, her elbows resting on the kitchen counter.

Mother added sugar to the bowl and said, "I hope your Great-aunty Hauty and Grandpère Hy enjoy my apple kugel."

"I don't know that they enjoy anything," said Lulu.

"Unfortunately, I must agree," said Harry, who had appeared on the countertop behind the mixing bowl.

Mother said, "That's an unkind thing to say."

Lulu watched the yolks and whites being twirled into a tempest. She didn't say anything.

"Yes, unkind," Mother said, beating at the eggs. Mother sometimes persisted in her thoughts, beating dead horses, so to speak. "Most unkind. They are, after all, gray-haired people set in their ways."

"Yes, Mother," said Lulu. She and Harry rolled their eyes at each other.

"Well! At any rate," said Mother. Whenever Mother said "Well!" with an exclamation point and "At any rate," it meant she was changing the subject. "You used to have a monster under your bed, when you were a little girl. Do you remember?" Mother said.

"Yes, I do," said Lulu.

"Wasn't that the very same monster that is under Master Sam's bed?" said Harry.

Lulu nodded.

"You were very young then, Lulu. My goodness, I haven't thought of that in ages! You were just like Sam! You got rid of him, didn't you?" said Mother, referring to the monster.

"I thought so," said Lulu.

"I had *hoped* so," added Harry.

"How?" asked Mother.

"I forget," said Lulu, telling the truth.

"Well, don't worry. Perhaps it will all come back to you, and you can get rid of Sam's monster the same way," said Mother.

"Perhaps," said Lulu.

"Perhaps," said Harry.

Neither Lulu nor Harry looked convinced.

"But I still say it's just a mouse!" said Mother, pouring flour. Some flour made it into the mixing bowl, but a good deal fell to the floor. Mother did a little soft-shoe in it and smiled.

"At least she can still smile," Lulu said to Harry as they left the kitchen to Mother and her baking. "She doesn't have a monster under *her* bed!"

The sun floated to the peak of the roof of Lulu's home, topping it off at noon. By midafternoon, the sun was sending lengthy black shadows of trees across the snowy yard. And by the time Mother, Lulu and Harry sat at the kitchen table to have their late-afternoon tea and hard-boiled eggs, it was growing dark.

Sam was napping in his bedroom. After the emotional turmoil of the morning, what with the monster and all, Sam was sleeping well. It was not until he heard the rustling coming from below, and felt the banging against the legs of his crib, that he stirred.

His entire crib shifted! It leaped away from the wall and landed a good inch out into the room.

"Yike!"

The crib shook. It vibrated and the metal bars on the sides clanked against the wooden slats.

"Yike! I said *YIKE!*" yelled Sam, hoping someone would hear him.

Sam looked out between the wooden slats. He looked down to the floor. His room was almost dark, but not dark enough for him to miss the hairy hand that was reaching out from beneath the crib.

"YOOOWWWLLLLLLL!!" Sam yowled.

Lulu rushed in. Harry rushed in. Mother rushed in.

"What is it, Sam?" Mother said, snatching up her baby and hugging him close.

"It's the monster," said Lulu. Harry clung to Lulu's leg, shivering.

"Did Sammy see a mousie?" said Mother, pecking him on his cheeks and nuzzling his neck with her nose.

Sam sniffled and rubbed his eyes. "Uh-huh," he said, nodding through his tears.

"Come with Mother and help fix things for the visit. Great-aunty Hauty and Grandpère Hy are almost here!" said Mother, far more cheerfully than need be.

Mother left the nursery with Sam in her arms. Lulu and Harry followed close behind. Lulu closed the door slowly and quietly, but firmly. As she closed it, she stuck her head back into the room, squinting through the gathering dusk, looking for the monster. She could see nothing, but she knew it was there, lurking in the murky light. Breathing heavily. And waiting.

CHAPTER FIVE

The house was filled with the warm and welcoming aroma of apple kugel. Mother had the radio on and it was playing old songs. The radio sang,

"Nothing's impossible, I have found.
For when my chin is on the ground, . . .
I pick myself up, dust myself off,
Start all over again!"

Lulu watched as Mother danced around the kitchen with Sam, getting him over his fears. Sam giggled.

Harry jumped up on Lulu's knee. "May I have this

dance?" he said. He swept his top hat off his head and bowed deeply.

Lulu held Harry in the palm of her hand, just as if he were a perfect hard-boiled egg. They danced around the kitchen with Mother and Sam.

"Don't lose your confidence if you slip,
Be grateful for a pleasant trip,
And pick yourself up, dust yourself off,
Start all over again."

Harry and Lulu twirled, and then Lulu spun her way over to Mother, to ask her to dance. It was at just that moment that the doorbell rang.

"It's them!" cried Mother, cheerfully.

"It's them," said Lulu, dismally.

"Indeed, it *is* them," said Harry, hanging his head.

"Yike!" said Sam.

Mother opened the front door with Sam still in her

arms. Sam looked at the old lady and the older gentle-man standing on his doorstep. His face contorted and he wailed at the top of his lungs.

"Well, that is quite a greeting," said Great-aunty Hauty, her nose raised high in the air. Her nose was always raised high in the air. She stalked into the house stiff as a rod, pushing past Mother and Sam. She stood in the middle of the hallway, covered with strings of pearls and bangles of gold and a big fur coat. She turned toward the elderly gentleman who was doddering along behind her, leaning heavily on a cane. He wore a black suit that was rather dusty, a heavy gold watch chain across his broad belly and a wide silk tie the color of overblown lilacs.

"TUT. A FINE HOWDJA-DO!" he yelled. Grand-père Hy always yelled. He was deaf as a doorknob but too vain to wear a hearing aid.

Please understand, these relatives were not your

common breed of relatives. Great-aunty Hauty and her father, Grandpère Hy, led what is referred to as Privileged Lives. They had grand houses and limousines driven by chauffeurs in fancy gold livery. They had plumes for their hats and peacocks in their yards and many diamonds for their fingers. Plus there was the fact that Great-aunty Hauty had never had children, and Grandpère Hy—well, it was so long since he had children of his own, he would no longer recognize a child if he fell over one.

"Great-aunty Hauty! Grandpère Hy! How wonderful to see you again!" said Mother.

"I expect this is Lulu Atlantis, almost fully grown," said Great-aunty Hauty, looking way, way, *way* down her nose at Lulu. She held her pearls to her throat with one hand and tilted Lulu's face up to hers with her other hand.

"Getting better-*looking*, I must say. But *why* she ever

named you Lulu Atlantis is beyond me," said Great-aunty. She dropped Lulu's face as if it had turned into a worm. Then she examined Sam. "And isn't this one adorable," she said, smiling a smile that seemed uncomfortable on her face.

"Thank you, Great-aunty. He's a good child," said Mother.

"Good children should be in their cribs. Asleep," said Great-aunty Hauty. (Please keep in mind, she had never had a child of her own, good, bad or otherwise.)

"But we have a special evening planned," said Mother. She led her guests into the living room.

Great-aunty Hauty sat stiffly on the couch. She patted the cushion next to her, signaling Lulu to sit down. Lulu set Harry in the palm of her hand and walked slowly to the couch. She sat on the very edge of the seat.

"If you sit any closer to the edge, you'll be sitting on the floor," said Harry.

"It's fine. Be quiet," said Lulu.

"Are you telling your Great-aunty Hauty to be quiet, child?" asked Great-aunty Hauty, sounding offended.

"No, Great-aunty. I was talking to Harry," said Lulu.

"Who is Harry?" said Great-aunty, looking all about.

"He's my best friend."

Great-aunty Hauty looked all around, up, down and sideways. "I see no best friend," she said.

"He's a spider, and not always easily seen," said Lulu, holding her palm out to show off her friend proudly.

Grandpère Hy peered hard into Lulu's hand. He shook his head fervently. "TUT, TUT," he yelled. "I SEE NO HARRY, LITTLE GIRL! HARRY'S ALL IN YOUR HEAD!" he roared.

"Whether Harry is or whether Harry is not . . . spiders are best when dead," said Great-aunty Hauty with conviction. "Dead and squashed flat! And that is that!"

Lulu looked down at Harry, but Harry had vanished, like the sound of the snap of your fingers, into thin air.

"Dinner's ready," said Mother, changing the subject.

The family had dinner in the dining room. Mother sat at the foot of the table, giving Grandpère Hy, man of the house on that evening, the head. Sam sat in his high chair beside Great-aunty Hauty. Mother thought this would be a treat for Great-aunty. Neither Sam nor Great-aunty seemed to share in this thought. Lulu sat opposite Great-aunty, between Mother and Grandpère. Harry reappeared with a smile plastered on his face. He sat on the table beside Lulu's plate.

"Grace, please, Lulu Atlantis," said Mother.

All at the table held their hands in front of them in the prayer position and bowed their heads, except for Lulu. She never bowed her head in prayer. She looked up through the ceiling and into heaven. She felt it important to see God eye to eye.

Lulu said the prayer that Harry had taught her. "God, thank you for the food and for the mother who cooks it. We ask that you keep us healthy and fit, and whatever else we need, we leave up to you to figure out for us."

"Who taught you that lovely prayer, Lulu Atlantis?" asked Great-aunty Hauty.

"Harry," said Lulu.

"HOW'S THAT?" yelled Grandpère, leaning over the table and dragging his tie through his soup. He cupped his ear with his hand, the better to hear.

Lulu repeated loudly, "Harry!"

"TUT, TUT. THERE IS NO HARRY!" yelled Grandpère Hy into his soup.

CHAPTER SIX

Just as the group was finishing Mother's apple kugel, a knock came at the kitchen door.

"I'll get that," said Mother.

Lulu followed Mother into the kitchen, not wanting to be left holding down the fort with Great-aunty and Grandpère in it.

Mother opened the door. Standing in the dark on the back porch was the Eggman.

"Why, hello there!" said Mother.

"Why, hello there!" said the Eggman.

"Did you figure out what True Blue Love is yet?" Lulu asked the Eggman.

The Eggman looked at Lulu and then at Mother. Then he looked out at the night sky and then down at the back-porch floor.

"Would you like hot chocolate?" asked Mother quickly.

"I would love hot chocolate," said the Eggman, stepping inside.

He handed Mother a carton. "Here's something for you 'cause you're always nice to me. One dozen of the best medium browns I ever gathered." The Eggman presented the box to Mother.

"Oh, thank you! How kind! I can put these to good use." Mother picked one egg out of the carton and held it.

"Look, Lulu. See how well an egg fits into the palm of your hand?" Mother jiggled her hand a bit so the egg danced around gently in it. "And inside, a surprise."

"An everyday surprise," said the Eggman happily.

"Please join us. We are having a visit with my Great-aunty Hauty and my Grandpère Hy," said Mother.

Mother let Lulu lead the Eggman into the dining room, while she stayed in the kitchen fixing his hot chocolate. He left a thin trail of short hay bits behind him as he walked, and a thick trail of smells from the farm.

Mother brought the Eggman his hot chocolate. She said to the group, "Shall we go to the living room? We have some wonderful entertainment planned, my children and I." In the living room, Mother sat Great-aunty Hauty on the couch. She sat the Eggman next to Great-aunty, who edged herself as far away from the Eggman as humanly possible, scrunching herself up into a ball deep in the corner recess of the couch. Grandpère was placed in an overstuffed chair opposite the couch.

"Er . . . have you been on a farm lately, Mr. . . . er . . . Mr.," stammered Great-aunty, sniffing the farm smell wafting off him.

"Name's Eggman, ma'am. And I'm on a farm every day of my life. Ma'am," he replied.

"Is that so?" said Great-aunty, peering way down her nose at him.

"Yes, ma'am," said the Eggman. He was polite, even when being polite was difficult.

"BE MORE COMFORTABLE SITTING IN THE KITCHEN, WOULDN'T YOU?" yelled Grandpère Hy to the Eggman. Grandpère Hy leaned over the cane that was standing between his knees. His hands were folded over its handle. He looked at the Eggman, fully expecting him to agree.

"I don't think so, sir, thank you. I'm fine here, thank you, sir," said the Eggman. "Thank you for thinking of my comfort, though, sir," he added.

"We are all where we want to be. Isn't that right?" said Mother. She smiled at the Eggman and then smiled at Lulu.

Lulu smiled at Mother and then turned to Great-aunty and Grandpère Hy. She stuck out her tongue.

"Lulu," Mother warned.

Mother placed Sam on the floor in front of the couch. She gave him his favorite saucepan and his favorite wooden spoon.

Lulu stood beside him with her comb wrapped in tissue paper.

Mother put on her ballet slippers. They were made of a lovely pink leather, so soft you would have thought they had previously been worn by a fairy, or a bird of paradise. The pink leather ballet slippers had pink satin ribbons, which Mother wrapped prettily around her ankles and finished off in dainty bows.

"Good heavens," said Great-aunty Hauty, looking aghast.

"TSSSK," tsked Grandpère.

The Eggman smiled, appreciative of the color pink

and the sound of tissue paper against a comb and the rattle of a wooden spoon on a saucepan. He slurped his hot chocolate with noisy sips.

"Good heavens," Great-aunty said again, eyeing the Eggman.

Grandpère said nothing. His deafness shielded him from hearing anyone slurp.

From his seat on the arm of the chair, Harry nodded at Lulu, giving the cue to begin. Lulu put the comb with its tissue paper in front of her lips. She blew and she played a lilting tune. She nodded at Sam.

Sam picked up his cue and started banging on his saucepan with his wooden spoon, as if the saucepan were a drum. He banged in perfect rhythm to Lulu's tune. They were well rehearsed, having done this often on a winter's evening.

In time with the beat, Mother took Ballet First Position, with her heels together and her toes pointed out. She went into Ballet Second Position, and then Third, and then she started leaping and pirouetting about the room.

A grand time was had by Lulu, Sam and Mother. The time for Great-aunty Hauty and Grandpère Hy, however, left much to be desired.

Great-aunty Hauty held her hands over her ears. "Enough!" she cried.

Grandpère shook his head and humpfed fitfully.

The Eggman smiled and clapped his hands to the beat. He looked at Mother and her children as if they were angels from heaven. He was having a ball.

Mother and her children continued with their performance. Most probably, it was the ruckus they made with their music and dancing that prevented them from hearing the cries of "Enough!" from Great-aunty and the "humpf"s from Grandpère.

They also did not hear the insistent banging on the door of Sam's nursery down the hallway. Banging!

Pounding! A huge crashing at the door, as if a monster inside were desperate to get out!

CHAPTER SEVEN

In the general din, only Harry heard the knocking. He scuttled frantically down the chair and up Lulu's pant leg and leaped onto her shoulder.

"The Monster!" he panted breathlessly into her ear. But Lulu was all wrapped up in her playing. Harry pulled on her hair. "The Monster!" he rasped, pointing down the hallway toward Sam's room. Still she didn't hear him.

The knocking became fiercer, but so did the music. And so did the dancing, until the walls of Lulu's home shivered and the floor wrung its hands. Finally Great-aunty jumped up off the couch. She strode over to Mother, reached out and grabbed her by the arm, right in the middle of a pirouette. She grabbed her so roughly, she knocked Mother for a loop. Mother fell over, bringing Great-aunty down with her. Together they knocked over the good antique table that Mother cherished.

"Oh!" said Mother.

"Oy!" said Great-aunty.

"HI!" yelled Grandpère Hy.

Lulu stopped playing. Sam stopped banging. The knocks on the nursery door stopped too, as if the monster had been shocked into silence.

"Whatever are you thinking? Are you a nut?" Great-aunty yelled at Mother.

"I am not a nut," said Mother.

"Indeed she is not!" said Harry from his perch on Lulu's shoulder.

"Don't call my mother a nut!" said Lulu.

"She isn't any nut, I tell you!" said the Eggman, leaping to his feet and beating the air with his fist.

"NOW!" cried Grandpère Hy, tapping his cane on

his way across the living room floor. "WHAT WE ALL NEED IS A GOOD NIGHT'S SLEEP! WE ALL NEED TO CALM DOWN AND GET A GOOD NIGHT'S SLEEP IS WHAT WE ALL NEED!"

Everyone took a deep breath. It was a very loud, group breath, all done at the same time. Together, all the deep breaths that were taken formed one breath so deep, the slipcovers on the sofa and the Persian scatter rugs, the china knickknacks on the mantel and the pages of the magazines were almost sucked into the lungs of those who took the deep breaths.

Great-aunty Hauty said in a voice that was measured, "A good night's sleep is just what we need. Of course, I'll expect to stay in the room with the western exposure," she added to Mother.

"The only room with a western exposure is Sam's nursery," said Mother. She chewed a lock of her dark hair nervously.

"A nursery!" said Great-aunty Hauty. "Most unsuitable for guests! But if there's no other way, the child will have to find alternate quarters. Come, let us see this nursery." Great-aunty Hauty stalked to the doorway of the living room that led into the hall. The others followed.

Mother called to Great-aunty Hauty's back, "Oh, no, Great-aunty. You wouldn't like Sam's nursery. I think there's a mouse in it."

"Nonsense. A mouse would never *dare* to enter my home," said Great-aunty.

"But it's *our* home," said Mother.

"Nonsense, child. *You* are related to *me*. And so it stands. A mouse would never *dare*. And I simply *must* have a western exposure. Otherwise, I am troubled by that ghastly early-morning sun. It is so *bright*, it is simply ostentatious! I do not want to be troubled by an ostentatious sun!"

"But—" said Mother.

"Good idea," said Lulu. "We'll move the cots into Sam's nursery." She grinned a mischievous grin and led the procession down the narrow hallway to Sam's nursery.

Just as the procession reached the closed nursery door, there came a good knock on it from the monster inside. The knock was so good, in fact, that the door rattled on its hinges. The adults clutched at their throats and stared at the door as if it had a life of its own. Then they looked elsewhere, silently deciding that they had imagined the knock.

"Are you sure you want them to stay in there?" Harry whispered.

"The nursery it will be, for them that called my mother a nut," said Lulu.

Lulu smiled at Mother.

"But—" Mother said.

Great-aunty Hauty interrupted Mother. "I *insist*

upon a western exposure. Open the door at once, if you please," she said.

CHAPTER EIGHT

Harry sat with Sam on the living room floor, watching him while he played with his saucepan. Sam played with his saucepan by putting it on his head and then swiveling his head violently back and forth inside it. Harry feared Sam would scramble his brains like eggs.

Lulu and the Eggman helped Mother set up the cots in the nursery.

When they were finished, the Eggman politely took his leave. He thanked one and all for a most enjoyable evening. Mother thanked him for the perfect medium browns.

"My pleasure," he said. "No bother 'tall."

As Mother and Lulu waved good-bye to the Egg-man, Lulu called out, "Can you get back to me on the True Blue Love issue?"

The Eggman smiled. "Will do!" he promised.

After the good-byes, it was time for bed. Everyone stood gathered at the nursery door.

The monster inside had quieted down since the door had been opened and the cots had been moved in.

"It's waiting," Lulu whispered to Harry.

Mother looked down at Lulu. "I hope it really is a mouse," she whispered.

"It's no-o-ot," Lulu sang back.

Great-aunty Hauty turned to Mother and said, "Good night." Grandpère Hy turned to Mother and bellowed, "GOOD NIGHT!" At that very moment, the pictures on the nursery wall began to shake and rattle and roll. At this very moment, the closet door within the nursery trembled and sighed and grew to a greater size, as if it had taken a deep breath. Then it seemed to exhale and shrank back to its normal size.

Neither Great-aunty Hauty and Grandpère Hy saw this, nor did they hear it. They were still looking at Mother with their backs to the room. However, Mother saw it and heard it, and so did Sam, Lulu and Harry.

"Yike," said Sam, relieved at being out in the hallway.

Mother said, "Oh, Great-aunty, you just *can't* sleep in there."

"Nonsense," said Great-aunty.

"Nonsense," said Lulu.

"Nonsense," said Harry.

Sam belched and laughed.

"Well, we'll all go in with you," said Mother, and escorted her guests into their room.

Great-aunty Hauty eyed Mother cradling Sam. "The boy is not staying in *here*, is he?" she said.

"No. Sam is sleeping with me tonight," said Mother.

Great-aunty sighed with relief.

So did Sam.

Lulu saw no monsters under the bed, and no mice. Only a few dust bunnies.

They said their good-nights and each went to his or her own bed.

Things were quiet.

For the time being.

Lulu could not get ahold of sleep, no matter how hard she tried. She closed her eyes, and her eyelids sprang back open, as if they had a mind all their own. She buried herself under comforters and blankets. She snuggled deep into the mattress and covered her head with her pillow.

But the thought kept creeping into her mind, of the monster oozing out from underneath Sam's crib and oozing over to the underneath of the cots on which rested Great-aunty Hauty and Grandpère Hy.

Giving up on catching even the slightest wink, Lulu sat up and threw back her covers. She tiptoed to her door and quietly opened it. She looked down the hallway to the nursery door. She heard the grandfather clock in the hallway chime. Midnight.

Midnight. That was when things happened. Midnight was when owls hooted and witches flew, when ghosts seeped like smoke through the keyhole in your door, and when your refrigerator gasped and sighed, tired of being cold. Midnight was when your house took on a life of its own, moaning at the burden of supporting so many chairs and sofas and humans and dogs and bathtubs and cats and cobwebs and hooked rugs and parakeets and mirrors. Not to even mention mice!

Lulu, shivering in her doorway, heard the knocking coming from the nursery. Mother, from her room, heard the rattling. Harry heard the whisperings and then the voices that made the hair on all eight of his legs stand on end. Mother and Harry and Sam all covered their heads with their blankets and squeezed their eyes tight, pretending to be asleep in case the monster should peek in their rooms to see what was up.

It was Lulu who ran on tiptoe to the nursery door. It was Lulu who put her hand on the door's haunted doorknob. It was Lulu who slowly opened the door, not knowing what to expect.

I must be honest. To this day, no one knows *exactly* what went on in that room on that dark, wintry night. But this much is known. At exactly thirteen minutes past midnight, shouts were heard from the nursery. They were so loud, they drowned out even the knocking and the rattling.

The nursery door slammed open and Lulu ran out, heading for her room to get Harry. She heard the nursery door slam shut behind her, and the voices of Great-aunty and Grandpère Hy.

"Oy!" cried Great-aunty.

"TUT! HOLD ON THERE AND TUT!" cried Grandpère Hy.

"C'mon, Harry!" Lulu called from the door.

"That's okay. I'll keep watch right here," said Harry.

"Come *on!*" said Lulu.

"Oh, all right," said Harry.

Mother jumped out of bed. "Stay!" she said to Sam, as if Sam were a dog being taught to obey a command.

Mother met Lulu and Harry at the nursery door.

"What is going on in there?" said Mother.

"I don't know," said Lulu.

Lulu was making ready to knock the door down if need be, when it swung open. Out ran a frantic Great-aunty Hauty. Her tightly waved, beautifully groomed gray hair was standing straight out from her head in crazy corkscrews. Her robe was on crooked, with the sash not around her waist but over one shoulder and under the other arm.

Out ran Grandpère Hy, not leaning on his cane but carrying it above his head. He swung it in great arcs. He was in his striped pajamas and his mouth was wide open, but no sound was coming out.

"We will send for our bags!" shouted Great-aunty Hauty.

"THANK YOU FOR A PLEASANT STAY!" shouted Grandpère Hy, remembering his manners.

"Where are you going?" shouted Mother after them.

"THE BUS STATION!" they shouted back.

Mother looked at Lulu and Lulu looked at Mother. Then she looked at Harry. By this time Sam, who did not quite understand the meaning of the command

"Stay," toddled out into the hall. He waddled over to Mother and held up his arms.

Mother picked Sam up and cuddled him close. She said, "What were you doing in there, Lulu?"

"I was just standing there. I was going to protect Great-aunty and Grandpère. I needed to," said Lulu.

"From a *mouse*?" said Mother.

"From a *monster*," said Lulu.

"Well, what happened?" said Mother.

"Well . . . there was . . . there was knocking! And rattling! The crib was shaking and standing up on its hind legs! There were pillows flying and mattresses and ugly shapes under the blankets, which, by the way, were *all over the floor*! Great-aunty's hair was all over the place and . . ." Lulu paused. She said, "I really don't know *what* went on in there."

Mother thought a moment. "Well, I think the mouse has been scared away by all this ruckus."

"I think the *monster* has been scared away . . . by Great-aunty Hauty and Grandpère Hy!" said Lulu.

"It's called fighting fire with fire," said Harry.

"It's called fighting monsters with monsters," said Lulu.

"Lulu Atlantis, do not be unkind," said Mother.

Lulu sighed.

While everyone was standing there looking at everyone else and wondering if they were indeed mouse- and monster-free, in the warm, moonlit, midnight hallway on that cold winter's night, no one noticed Yogurt Skunk slinking silently out through the nursery door.

No one but Lulu Atlantis, that is.

Lulu saw the huge, satisfied grin on his face. A smile that started small but grew quite large spread across her own face. A warmth spread through her body from the vicinity of her heart, and for the first time in many days, Lulu felt glad. She thought of the grace Harry had taught her: "We ask that you keep us healthy and fit, and whatever else we need, we leave up to you to figure out for us." And she thought that truly, Someone *had* figured out the thing she needed. Someone had returned her friend.

And Yogurt Skunk saw Lulu. He watched her smile. He caught her eye. Then Yogurt Skunk winked, and Lulu winked back.

Yogurt Skunk ran silently through the front door, which was still open after the guests' sudden departure. As he scrambled silently down the porch steps, he laughed to himself. *What a trick!* he thought. *What a splendid joke! That'll teach her to kick me out into the world!* Then he thought of the winks he and Lulu had exchanged. *Back to normal with my friend,* he thought, and sighed contentedly.

As he headed down the midnight lane, past nesting birds trying to get a good night's sleep, Skunk sang,

"Work like a soul inspired
Till the battle of the day is done.
You may be sick and tired,
But you'll be a man, my son.
Oh, nothing's impossible, I have found,
For when my chin is on the ground,
I pick myself up, dust myself off,
Start all over again."

part four
True Blue Love

CHAPTER ONE

The cat descended through clouds at night,
Descended through silver stars,
Drifted past Venus and Mars,
Sifted through music from

Fine steel guitars—
A cat, in her marmalade flight.

The cat descended from skies
To fields lit by fireflies,
Humming with tunes from valiant magpies,
Grass waving in breezes that
Sounded like sighs—
A cat, in her marmalade flight.

Her feet had golden boots
With rubies at their toes.
Her ears had golden earrings,
A diamond pierced her nose.
On her forehead, a red tattoo,
A crimson crescent moon,
And across her golden face, a smile
Sharp as a steel harpoon.

A Princess from another world,
A Princess! it was told
From a world with glitterflies
And oak trees made of gold;
It would be hard, be difficult
To make her happy here.
The family that found
This feline
Might well have things
To fear.

"We're in trouble now, Lulu Atlantis," said Harry. "What do you mean?"

"I don't know how we're going to deal with that cat," said Harry. His frail body shuddered and he choked back a sob.

"I've never seen you so upset," said Lulu.

"A cat would *never* be my first choice for a suitable

companion. If you know what I mean," said Harry, shaking his head in forlorn resignation. "Isn't it enough I have to deal with the likes of that Yogurt Skunk? Now I have to deal with this pompous, spider-devouring *feline*?" Harry pulled at the tight starched collar at his neck. He loosened his bow tie and wiped his forehead with his pressed white hankie.

"I am unfamiliar with the habits of cats," said Lulu. It was true. In all her life, Lulu had never had a cat.

"Let me tell you about the habits of *cats*!" Harry spat. "They are feral felines! Creatures of evil! Of that I can assure you." He worked worriedly at the wrists of his gloves.

"She can't be that bad," said Lulu. "Mother adopted her. Mother loves her. Mother's not stupid. Distracted, maybe, but certainly not stupid!"

Harry looked quizzical. "Poor Mother did not adopt *her*! The cat foisted herself upon us! Simply *foisted*!"

Lulu was as unfamiliar with the meaning of the word *foisted* as she was unfamiliar with the habits of cats, but she felt, when taken in context, *foisted* could not be interpreted as a good thing.

"Don't worry, Harry. We'll make out just fine. I think she's kind of cute. And furry. And . . . and . . ."

"And apparently *my* services are no longer required in this household!" said Harry. He stomped off, each one of his eight feet making a statement on the wood floor as he left.

Lulu sighed. She had seen Harry in similar huffs before, and felt that this one would subside with time.

Lulu was wrong. Harry's huff did not subside with time. On the contrary, with time it grew, just as lies or untended fears grow.

Harry was correct in one thing, if in nothing else. Mother had *not* adopted the marmalade fancy cat. The marmalade fancy cat had adopted Mother. The cat had simply moved in and taken over.

In she had waltzed, this marmalade fancy cat, right out of the blue and into their yard, right up the front steps to the front door, which was used only by the most honored and distant of family and acquaintances, and by strangers who had lost their way.

Mother had taken one look at the cat, with her long, soft orange fur and her fancy doodads (the golden boots and the golden earrings and the gemstones sparkling here and there, not to mention the blue satin bow at the tail), and had put her hands to her cheeks and gushed, "Oooooooooooooooooo!"

"She's never gushed like that in her life," Lulu said to Sam.

Sam hadn't heard. His eyes were filled with the marmalade fancy cat, brimming with delight at the picture of this bejeweled feline, this Beauty! this Dazzler! this Queen!

"Oooooooooooooooo!" said Sam.

Lulu had looked at Harry, ready to exchange meaningful glances with him as she often did. But Harry was not looking at her. He was looking at the marmalade fancy cat and he was bug-eyed. His very *teeth* chattered.

"What's the matter, Harry?" Lulu had asked.

In response, he'd turned on his heel—well, *all* his heels—and headed for the hills. Lulu would not see Harry again for several hours. And it was when he had returned from the hills, having decided that he needed to face his fate if he wanted to stay beside his True Blue Friend Lulu, that Harry made his comment: "We're in trouble now, Lulu Atlantis."

CHAPTER TWO

Mother gave the marmalade fancy cat milk in a crystal glass on a pedestal.

"Why are you using the good glass on the pedestal?" asked Lulu. The good glasses on the pedestals were used only for revered guests, like Great-aunty Hauty and Grandpère Hy.

"Stemware, Lulu. Crystal stemware. And I'm using it because this *marvelous* marmalade fancy cat deserves nothing less. Why, just *look* at her, Lulu Atlantis!" said Mother. She held out her arms toward the cat, her hands spread open as if presenting the cat to the world. "Isn't she just the bees' knees?"

The cat, hearing herself spoken of thusly, preened and held her proud head up high. She smirked at Lulu. She smirked at Sam. She peered at them coldly with her golden eyes. Then she turned her marmalade head slowly toward Mother and smiled, showing all her teeth. Confident. Composed. Dauntless. This was a cat who knew what side her bread was buttered on, that much I can tell you.

The cat waltzed herself over to the crystal stemware and lapped daintily at the milk—milk that had originally been intended for Sam.

"That's Sam's milk. It's *whole* milk. The rest of us get the two-percent," said Lulu. She made a face at the thought of the two-percent. She would have loved to have creamy whole milk.

"Obviously this poor cat has come from afar. She needs her energy," said Mother. She bent over and smoothed the golden fur along the cat's back. She tickled the cat's ears, being careful not to disturb the golden earrings. She tickled the cat's paws, being careful not to make fingerprints on the golden boots.

The cat tolerated Mother's caresses.

Lulu persisted. "Sam," she said to her little brother, "that cat's lapping up *your* milk. Now you'll be stuck with the two-percent, like the rest of us."

But Sam sat mesmerized, watching the marmalade fancy cat, falling head over heels in love.

"A cat wearing such precious jewelry, not to mention the beautifully tied bow, must belong to someone. I am calling the cat warden," said Mother.

Harry, who had crept up onto Lulu's shoulder and was hiding in her long hair, cried, "Yahoo! The cat warden! That's just the ticket!" And he sighed a sigh of relief.

Lulu, eyeing the empty glass on the pedestal, eyeing the looks of foolish infatuation on the faces of Mother and Sam, eyeing the cold demeanor of this overdressed cat, was inclined to agree.

"Stupid cat!" said Lulu.

"Don't be unkind," said Mother, dialing up the cat warden.

They waited several days, but no one claimed the cat. Well, who would? Who would claim a cat who had fallen from the sky? A cat who made a practice of *foisting* herself?

The warden, sitting in an office filled to the ceiling with unwanted cats mewling about, called Mother on the phone.

"Guess she's yours, if you want her. Hope you *do* want her! I'm up to my neck in felines around here," he said.

"Oh, yes!" gushed Mother. "We would *love* her!" Mother's smile started on one side of her head and wrapped itself completely around her face to the other side.

"Fancy," said Mother. "We will name her Princess Fancy."

Lulu turned and walked away. She said to Harry, still hidden in her hair, "No way am I calling it Princess."

"I agree," said Harry. "That feline would *never* make a good princess. It's obviously of very poor breeding."

The cat, who sat in the sunlight in a window, bathing herself and polishing her jewels, suddenly turned her pointed face to Harry. She squinted evilly and hissed and spoke in low growls.

"I'm *hungry*," snarled Princess Fancy. She growled a

growly laugh deep in her throat. *"Hungry,"* she said once again. She broadened her grin, showing Harry her sharpened fangs sparkling with drool.

"Why is it I'm invisible to virtually everyone else on this planet, and not to that *feline?"* moaned Harry.

"Them's the breaks," said Lulu, rather unfeelingly.

CHAPTER THREE

It is late in our story, and we still have the problem of Lulu's Quest. After all, it is the theme of this entire book, and yet Lulu felt as if she hadn't gotten anywhere in her search for True Blue Love. True Blue Love was being rubbed in her face every time she turned around . . . for everyone else, that is! Where was hers?

Sam had a True Blue Love. It was evident in the way he traipsed after Princess Fancy, in the way he gave her his whole milk—even though that meant he was stuck with the two-percent. It was evident in the way he tried to pet her. She would swipe at him, scratching him with her claws so deeply she drew blood, and he would just smile, and his eyes would twinkle.

Mother certainly had *her* fair share of True Blue Love. *More* than her fair share! She'd already had Sam, and now she had *that cat.* Mother followed the cat around, brushing her fur, straightening the blue bow on her tail. She spent money buying the cat whole milk and, when Princess Fancy sneezed at the whole milk . . . *cream!*

"She only gets cream for *us* on Memorial Day, for the strawberry shortcake," said Lulu. "What's with the cream? What is she, a millionaire all of a sudden?"

Even Harry had True Blue Love, although not with Princess Fancy, of course. Harry's True Blue Love was Lulu. It was evident in the way he stuck by her through thick and thin, storms and fair weather, scary gangsters, Yogurt Skunks, and spider-devouring marmalade fancy cats.

"I think you're being just plain dumb, Harry. With that cat around, you're always in danger. She could zap you in a second: smack, scoop, crunch and squish! Any time, any place. You're a goner if you stay around here," Lulu said. "If I were you, I'd pack my suitcase and make a beeline for the bus station!"

"But wouldn't you miss me, miss?" asked Harry.

Lulu shrugged. She hung her head and stared hard at the floor. "Just get out while you can," she murmured.

"And leave you?" Harry asked.

Lulu sighed and then gave Fancy a look. A glower, in fact. Deep and dark and meaningful.

Fancy was not put off, not at all. She simply glowered back and chuckled her growly, odious chuckle. She gave a pompous tilt to her head and then turned to her rubies and her diamond, polishing them to an icy sparkle.

Lulu saw Harry shudder.

Lulu thought of all those around her who happily gave up things, important things, for someone else. Lulu wondered: Would *she* willingly give up her food for someone else? Would she spend her very last penny on cream for someone else? And what about Sam? How much of herself would she give for her only brother? At that moment, Lulu realized that people who found True Blue Love were people who were unselfish and openhearted. And it was also at that moment, and with that realization, that Lulu knew she would never experience True Blue Love.

Lulu went looking for Mother. She found her kneeling in the garden, digging with a trowel. She was transplanting a clematis vine. Its feet were not getting enough shade. Its head was not getting enough sunshine.

Lulu knelt down facing her mother. She said, "Mother, what exactly is True Blue Love?"

"True Blue Love? Let's see, now . . . ummmm . . ."

"Don't you know?"

"Well . . ." Mother scratched her head with the trowel. Clumps of dirt fell on her hair.

"Father could tell me what True Blue Love is. Right off the bat!" Lulu pointed out.

"Of course he could," Mother said, and smiled.

"But Father's not here."

"I'm sure," said Mother, rather distractedly. She was focusing on the feet of the clematis, trying to make them comfy under their blanket of soil.

"Mother!"

"What?"

"Could you pay attention? To *me*?"

"Oh, Lulu, I'm sorry, dear." Mother remained

crouched at the clematis's feet, but she stopped working. She put down her trowel, folded her gloved hands on her knees and looked hard at Lulu. "Now. You have my undivided attention. Talk to me," she said, leaning toward Lulu with a warm smile.

"All right. It's about this True Blue Love thing. Since Father isn't here, I've had to figure it out for myself. And this is what I figure. *I'm* never going to have True Blue Love, never! How could I? True Blue Love comes to people who do good for others. They give and they give and they never care about *themselves*, only about the *other* people. And look at me! I ran away just because you had Sam. I told my Frog Prince I was going to eat him. I clobbered Yogurt Skunk with a broom and threw him out of my life. *I blew at Harry!* Oh, I've shot my chance for True Blue Love, that's for sure!" Lulu said. Her eyes turned red and glassy and her throat constricted. She gulped, trying to hold in the tears.

"Now you're talking crazy!" said Mother, putting

her hands on her hips. "You're *always* doing things for others. Look at the lovely gifts you brought to Sam, the mulberries from your Umbrella Tree, that fine sunshine-spider cookie you baked yourself, the gold bracelet! And look at all the things you do for *me*! You gave me a break and fixed Sam his breakfast. And you went to a lot of trouble for *that*, I might add! Look how you wait in the freezing cold for the Eggman to get my eggs. Look how you tried to help Great-aunty Hauty and Grandpère Hy with the monster . . . er . . . the mouse. Oh, Lulu, if only you could see what *I* see!" With that, Mother leaned over and cupped Lulu's chin in her gloved hands, streaking that chin with soil. Then she sat back on her heels, picked up her trowel and pounded the ground with it, tamping down earth over the clematis's roots.

"I miss Father," Lulu said quietly.

"I know you do, dear. We all do." Mother put down her trowel once again and took Lulu's hands in hers.

"Will he be back soon?" asked Lulu, sniffling.

Mother looked into her daughter's red eyes and said, "Your father goes where life takes him. And he'll come home when his job is done, with wonderful stories for us. When exactly that will be, I just don't know."

Lulu withdrew her hands from Mother's, gently but with finality. Her chin sank to her chest and she stared hard at the soil in which Mother had been digging.

Mother said softly, "What are you thinking, sweetheart?"

Lulu shrugged, then sniffled. "I'm thinking . . . well, that if Father were here, he'd tell me the answers. I'd have *all* the answers, if Father were here."

"There are some questions that we must find answers to on our own."

"Do you think True Blue Love is one of them, Mother?"

"I do."

"I feel alone."

"If you take the time to think, you'll find that lots of people care about you, Lulu Atlantis."

Lulu just kept on looking at the soil covering the feet of the clematis. She didn't say anything.

After Mother finished with the clematis, she went in to fix the drain in the kitchen sink. As she stepped up the steps to the back porch, she turned and looked over her shoulder at Lulu. "I love you," she said, and waited a moment for Lulu to respond. When she didn't, Mother turned and went into the house.

Lulu stayed still as a stone, kneeling in the garden.

Lulu remained in the garden, isolated amid the zinnias.

"I think you're shortchanging yourself," said someone.

The clematis, looking relieved at being in a place

where his feet would be properly shaded and his head would receive the proper amount of sunshine, had a single purple flower. It was the flower that had spoken.

Harry sat on the clematis vine close by the purple flower.

"We are in agreement on this, Clematis and I," said Harry, nodding toward the flower. "You are not giving yourself credit where credit is due, miss." Harry and the clematis flower nodded at each other.

Fancy came out to the garden and smirked at Lulu.

"What do *you* want?" said Lulu.

"Everything," Fancy purred. *"Everything,"* she growled.

A dark cloud blew itself across the sun and stopped all the warm rays from getting to Earth. Harry had disappeared and the single clematis flower had folded in upon itself. Lulu shivered.

CHAPTER FOUR

"Rise and shine!" Mother sang.

"What time is it?" said Lulu. Her voice was muffled. She had buried her head under her pillow at the first sound of Mother entering her room.

"It's time to rise and shine! Today is a special day," said Mother.

That day, the family was to have a picnic on the shore of Lake George, at the foot of Bear Foot Falls. Bear Foot Falls was the tall waterfall that poured from Dead Man's Creek, which ran along the top of Black Mountain. Ordinarily a picnic in that spot was the family's favorite thing to do.

"So why is your face hanging down to your shoes?" asked Harry.

"Because of the *reason* for this picnic. That feline has been with us for two months today. This picnic is its anniversary party," said Lulu. "Like we're all thrilled!"

"Mother's idea?" asked Harry.

"Mother's idea," said Lulu.

"Look, toots, if I were you, I'd relax and have a grand old time. Who cares if it's a party for that cat, anyway? Just ignore Miss Fancypants and have fun!" said Yogurt Skunk. He had been outside in the garden eating his breakfast of click beetles and grubs. Now he hung over Lulu's windowsill, munching on something slimy and green. "Mmmmm," he said, polishing it off and picking his teeth with the leg of a beetle.

"I agree," said Harry. "We'll don our best duds and make a great day out of it."

"I have a bad feeling," said Lulu.

"Well, at least you're feeling something!" said

Yogurt Skunk. Everyone had noticed the decline in Lulu's enthusiasm these days.

"I'll pick a rosebud for my lapel and a rose for your hair," said Harry. He skittered to the door and, looking both ways for that cat, skittered down the hall and out of sight.

Princess Fancy's second-month anniversary happened to fall on the same day as the famous, world-renowned, nearby Extraordinary All-American Hot-Air Balloon Festival.

"Wait until Sam sees those balloons," said Mother.

Sam was in his car seat at one end of the backseat of Mother's car, kicking his feet in anticipation. "Balloons, balloons," he crooned to Princess Fancy, who was stretched out across the middle of the backseat, lying like Cleopatra on a fainting couch. He tried to tickle her ears, but she swiped him with her nails. Sam smiled and crooned to her some more.

Lulu whipped her head around and leaned into Fancy's face. "Don't you touch him, you . . . you . . . *feline!*" Lulu warned in a threatening whisper, so Mother wouldn't hear.

Mother heard anyway. "Lulu, be nice," she said.

Lulu backed farther into the corner of the backseat, where she sat cramped under a pile of picnic blankets, the picnic basket, beach towels, bottles of lotion, and magazines for Mother, and Sam's diaper bag with its many diapers and wet wipes.

Please understand, the balloons of the Extraordinary All-American Hot-Air Balloon Festival were not your ordinary run-of-the-mill red and yellow and green and orange and purple party balloons, the kind that do nothing but get detached from your hand and float away to nowhere. These were balloons as big as houses. They had large wicker baskets attached to their bottoms. People stood in the baskets and let the balloons take them for glorious rides up, up into the blue sky. The people in the baskets waved down at those below them, and the people down below waved up at the people floating away.

"Our picnic spot is directly in the path of the Hare and Hounds Balloon Race," said Mother, backing the car out of the driveway a bit faster than usual. The radio was turned on to lively music, a bit louder than usual.

"The balloons will undoubtedly pass right over our heads," said Harry. Harry sat in Lulu's pocket. He kept several hands cupped over his rosebud for fear of getting it crushed. It was hot in the pocket, but he'd rather be hot than run the risk of being the feline's picnic lunch.

Mother drove her car toward Lake George. Close behind was another car, a rusty green jalopy. The Eggman followed Mother to the lake. Atop his car he carried several dozen eggs, both large whites and medium browns. He drove slowly, calling out, "Eggs. Buy your eggs from the Eggman! Buy your eggs from me!"

"Why not do a little business, even on my day off?" he asked the passengers in his car.

"You ain't kiddin', Egg!" the passengers all agreed. They were Yogurt Skunk, Gangster Baker Lefty-Righty Louie, Gangster Baker Scarecrow and Gangster Pastry Chef Jimmy Creamcheese, all sprawled about like dandies. The gangsters were sporting their new silver top hats, which glistened like dewy cobwebs in the early sun.

Mother parked the car. She and Lulu lugged the blankets and the picnic basket, Sam's diaper bag and Sam's wet wipes, the beach towels and the bottles of lotion and Mother's magazines up the hill to a sunny spot near Bear Foot Falls. Sam followed, clinging to the hem of Mother's skirt.

"Can you carry Princess Fancy, Lulu? I think the hill may be too steep for her," said Mother.

"I'm full up, Mother. The feline will have to fend for itself," said Lulu, blowing the hair off her forehead.

"*Herself*," said Mother.

"I carry," said Sam. He reached out toward the cat. He wiggled his fingers in a come-hither gesture to Princess Fancy.

Princess Fancy glanced at Mother to make sure she wasn't looking. Then Fancy bared her teeth at Sam, hissed at Lulu and sprang up the hill easily on her own. Her jewels sparkled in the morning sun and her fur glistened.

"Is she a thing of beauty or what?" gushed Mother, who turned around in time to see the cat run up the hill, but not to see her bare her teeth.

Lulu felt Harry move in her shirt pocket, right over her heart. "Yeah. She's *something*, all right," she said.

By that time, the Eggman had pulled his car up next to Mother's, and his passengers scattered into the park like grains of sand in the wind.

CHAPTER FIVE

The Eggman helped Mother and Lulu spread the picnic blanket out, and they placed the picnic basket on top. They set Sam's diaper bag aside and took his shorts off. His bathing trunks were on underneath, with his diaper underneath those.

Seeing that it was still early morning, they started out their picnic with bagels. The Eggman offered deviled eggs.

"Why'd we have to come so early?" asked Lulu.

"The Hare and Hounds race happens early in the

morning, Lulu. You don't want to miss the Hare and Hounds!" said Mother.

"I've never missed the Hare and Hounds in all my years," said the Eggman.

Harry peeked out of Lulu's pocket. No sign of the cat. He jumped down onto the picnic blanket and helped himself to a crumb from Lulu's bagel.

"Where's the feline?" he said.

Lulu shrugged and shook her head.

"The day's turning out well, don't you think, miss?" Harry said.

"Time will tell."

"Those teenagers are jumping off the top of the falls again," said Mother. "I hope they're careful." She watched the big kids off in the distance. They stood at the top of Bear Foot Falls and dove straight down into the depths of Lake George.

"I did that too, as a kid," said the Eggman.

"You cannot tell teenagers anything these days," said

Harry to Mother. Mother pursed her lips but did not reply.

"It's dangerous up there," Mother continued. "Dead Man's Creek runs strong. The rocks are slippery. If you're not a strong swimmer and you get pulled along the creek and over the falls . . . you might as well forget it!" Mother shivered.

"Look! A balloon!" shouted the Eggman, pointing to the sky.

Mother hopped up from the blanket. "A *beautiful* balloon!" she cried, clapping her hands.

Sure enough, a single balloon came floating out of the blue. It glittered in the sun, as if lit with thousands of fairy lights.

"Talk about things of beauty!" Mother exclaimed.

"Talk about joys forever!" said Harry. He jumped off Lulu's knee. "Balloons!" he shouted.

Lulu watched quietly.

Mother said, "Where is Princess Fancy? I haven't

seen her since we got here." And then, in a voice filled with fear, she cried, "Where is Sam?"

The Eggman jumped up beside Mother. Harry skittered to the edge of the picnic blanket.

"Sam!" they all called at once. *"Sam!"*

Lulu froze. She sat like a statue on the picnic blanket, her eyes wide and unseeing.

Mother ran frantically in circles, bumping into the Eggman and almost stomping on Harry. Lulu did not move.

"LULU!" Mother screamed again. *"Help us!"*

With that, Lulu thawed. Still seated on the blanket, she turned her head, as if in slow motion, up to the jutting boulders that sat under the surging, churning deluge that was Bear Foot Falls. Lulu raised her arm and pointed.

Sam was standing at the very edge of Dead Man's Creek. He was watching the older kids jump and cavort and laugh. Sam laughed with them. They didn't notice him. They brushed past Sam, knocking him over. And there was Sam rolling down the hill, picking himself up and toddling back up to watch once again.

"SAM!" Mother screamed. She charged up the hill, her dark hair flying out behind her. At her heels was the Eggman.

Lulu flew past Mother and past the Eggman, with Harry chasing close behind her.

Sam toddled closer and closer to the edge of Dead Man's Creek. He was soaked from the spray of the falls. His feet slid on the slippery rocks.

Lulu ran faster than she'd ever run.

"Miss! Lulu! Watch the rocks!" shouted Harry, who should never, ever in his life have gone close to water that surged, that sprayed so fiercely! Never, ever should have been so near charging currents, soaking sprays, big kids running rampant!

"Stay back, Harry! It's bad up here!" screamed Lulu.

"LULU ATLANTIS! *YOU CAN'T SWIM!*" Harry cried.

Just as she got to the top of the hill, Lulu saw Sam stumble and slide. She saw him fall into Dead Man's Creek.

Lulu heard Sam scream.

Lulu knew she couldn't swim very well. She remembered Mother saying, "If you're not a strong swimmer . . . forget it!" Lulu heard Harry call from somewhere behind her, "*YOU CAN'T SWIM!*" But none of this stopped Lulu. She charged wildly ahead, and through her mind ran these words . . . *Sam! My Sam!*

Lulu jumped over the rocks and crashed into the water. She kept her eyes on Sam, who was bobbing. Then he disappeared.

Sam! Underwater! The buzzing of millions of bumblebees filled Lulu's ears. Her head felt as if it were filled with helium.

Water surged about her, dragging her after Sam toward the crest of the falls. Instead of fighting the current, Lulu pushed herself along with it. She bobbed up—she sank down! She submerged and resurfaced, choking on water, gasping for breath!

She reached and grabbed the back of Sam's shirt, yanked him to her, as they both careened over the crest of the falls.

CHAPTER SIX

It was at exactly that moment—*exactly*—that the hot-air balloon floated past. It skimmed the crest of the falls. Lulu looked up as she and Sam went over. The basket, which was covered with garlands of crystal drops and twinkling with pink fairy lights, carried a single passenger.

Princess Fancy.

Princess Fancy stood tall in the basket, grinning and

waving to those below, as the Queen of Sheba would have waved to her loyal subjects.

Lulu reached out as far as she could possibly reach . . . no, actually, *farther* than she could possibly reach. Lulu *flew*. She used the air as a springboard. She grunted! strained! arched her back! grabbed the basket of the hot-air balloon with one hand. She clutched Sam close to her heart with the other. She held on for dear life.

The balloon floated past Bear Foot Falls and out over Lake George. Lulu clung to the basket; Sam clung to Lulu. Dangling dangerously down, they swayed high in the air.

The last thing Lulu heard was the tiny voice of Harry, who screamed her name over and over. "LULU LULU LULU LULU . . ."

Lulu snapped her head around in the direction of Harry's voice. She saw him reach out to her, slip on the rocks and plunge headlong past the trees and into the falls. He disappeared in the raging spray, leaving what looked like a thin silver thread arcing behind.

"HARRY!" Lulu screamed.

Lulu felt needles in her right hand, the hand that held tight to the basket. Needles and pins. Forcing her face away from the lake, away from Harry, she looked up.

Fancy bent over the rim of the basket, grinning, pricking and digging at Lulu's hand with her claws. And she growled down deep in her throat, "There's room for only *one* princess in that house. And you're looking at her. So long!" And Princess Fancy clawed Lulu's hand deeply and painfully with all her claws.

The pain was too great. Lulu had to let go of the basket. Still clutching Sam to her chest, she dropped down, down, down into the cold water of the lake.

CHAPTER SEVEN

In the days after the tragedy at Bear Foot Falls, things changed at the house on Sweet Pea Lane. Mother tended to Lulu and Sam as if they were the last remaining humans on the face of the planet. She gave them whole milk to drink and strawberries drenched in sugar and cream to eat, even though strawberries were out of season and therefore very expensive.

Lulu did not ask Mother, "What are you, a millionaire?" Nor did she drink her whole milk. Her strawberries in sugar and cream withered and soured in their bowl.

Sam stuck to Lulu like glue. He followed her into the kitchen and out of the kitchen, into the living room and out of the living room, from one room to another, and then back again. Lulu had not been out of doors since the day of the tragedy.

Lulu noticed that Mother did not seem to mind seeing her son follow her daughter around like a shadow. In fact, Mother took to commenting, "How nice that you two are always together. It makes it far easier for me to care for you both!"

Mother sat on Lulu's bed, where Lulu lay with Sam curled at her side. Sam played within the little circle of himself, drawing lines and poking dots into the bedsheet with his finger. He sighed and looked lovingly at Lulu. Lulu stared at the wall and then at the ceiling and then at the wall again. The expression on her face never changed.

Mother gently tickled their ears and played with their fingers. She tickled their toes. It was as if she were counting everything, making sure all was well, all was safe.

During those days, as Mother tended to her children in Lulu's room, Princess Fancy remained in other parts of the house.

The princess had appeared at the kitchen door all by herself the night after the tragedy, and had let herself in. She had spent the night polishing her jewels, trying to get them back to their former shine.

The next morning, she noticed a severe chill in the air. She took to roaming from one window to another. There was no sunshine warm enough for her. There was no longer fresh cream in her dish. The residue of the old cream had hardened into a smelly, yellowed ring in the crystal. Mother had forgotten to clean it. In fact, Mother had forgotten all about her.

Fancy grew hungry, but she refused to stoop to the level of a common earth cat and actually hunt mice.

The mice of the house sighed in relief.

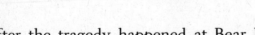

After the tragedy happened at Bear Foot Falls, after Mother, the Eggman and the Lake George rescue people had pulled Lulu and Sam out of the lake,

Yogurt Skunk and the gangsters of the Gangsters' Bakery had gathered up the diaper bag and the wet wipes, the picnic blanket and the picnic basket, the beach towels and the bottles of lotion and Mother's magazines. They had carried it all to Lulu's house. Then each had returned to his work. They held moments of silence and said short prayers during their workdays for Lulu and for Sam, and for the dear departed.

Yogurt Skunk abandoned the kitchen garden.

"My appetite ain't what it used to be," he said, if anyone asked. He sat in the driveway, watching for someone who might just come home, who might just magically appear at the end of the drive, waving his top hat, fiddling with the wrists of his white gloves, and skittering up to the house.

"To what end?" said Clematis to him. "For what purpose? You know he can never come back."

Yogurt Skunk said nothing.

CHAPTER EIGHT

It is odd how hollow a house can feel after the removal of something so small, so light, something that measures no more than an inch and a half in diameter, something that weighs no more than an ounce! How empty, how silent, how dispirited a home can become after the removal of something that is not even visible to everyone in the house.

It is also odd how flat a person can become when her spirit leaves her. Lulu Atlantis looked as flat as a page in a prayer book, as thin as the skin of an onion. It seemed that she was actually disappearing, that you could see through her, to the bed and the bureau beyond.

Such was the state of affairs in the house on Sweet Pea Lane.

CHAPTER NINE

Since no body had been recovered from the churning maelstrom of the lake at the foot of Bear Foot Falls, there could be no funeral. Lulu planned a memorial service instead, to be held at twilight, when the fireflies flickered over the high grasses and in the thin branches of the trees. The service was to be held directly in front of the Umbrella Tree.

Lulu went down to the Umbrella Tree to prepare for it. Bravely, she faced the fact that she might have to confront that fierce, ugly, hairy mother spider with the ugly, hairy baby spider who resided inside.

Lulu was right. The spider was there, in no better mood than when Lulu had first run into her so long ago (a lifetime ago!), when Lulu and Harry had first run away.

"You have to clear out!" Lulu said to the ugly spider.

"Says who?" spat the ugly spider.

"Says me!" spat Lulu right back, poking her own chest with her thumb. She glared at the spider.

"Oh, all right, then," said the ugly spider, tsking but backing down quickly. Then, to save face, she said, "I was going to move anyway. I'm moving *up* in the world. This place is a dump!"

Lulu prepared the ground in front of the Umbrella Tree for the memorial service. She clipped the grass with garden shears and raked away the clippings. She swept away the ugly spider's cobwebs and rearranged the branches so that they hung gracefully. She made a circular fence out of Popsicle sticks. Inside the circle, she set a pot of Mother's red geraniums. To several of the petals she pasted top hat silhouettes that she had cut out of black construction paper.

Later at home, Sam toddled close behind Lulu out into the garden. Lulu picked them each a stem of white phlox for their lapels. Sam held on to the tail of her shirt and would not let go.

Mother complimented Lulu on her choice of flower for the service. "White is the color of eternal life," said Mother. "Of living forever."

Lulu invited everyone to come.

When the sun cast long shadows across the field, when the starlings were settling into their nests and the foxes were nestled in their dens, when the air had turned from gold to pewter, they gathered at the Umbrella Tree.

There was Mother in a fine dress of white silk. There was Sam in his best Sunday shorts and a button-down shirt. His sprig of phlox covered his entire chest, it was so grand a sprig. Lulu wore a tuxedo and a top hat. She had gone to Lefty-Righty Louie, who seemed to know where to get his hands on anything that was ever to be desired by anyone. Her flower covered her heart.

The Eggman stood next to Mother. He wore brown dress pants and a tweedy jacket, the clothes he kept for holidays and for serious occasions.

The gangster bakers from the Gangsters' Bakery stood in a straight row, shoulder to shoulder. They each wore a black suit, a black shirt, a white tie and their silver cobweb top hats. There is much to be said for their attire, for it showed the respect the gangsters held for this sad occasion. Scarecrow's suit had hardly a splatter of icing on it, just a bit of yellow hanging off the sleeve. Chef Jimmy Cream-cheese had moved all his jacket buttons over to make his jacket an inch or two wider. He didn't want his beefy belly to pop any of the buttons off. And Lefty-

Righty Louie had starched even his socks and his hat, so that he was stiff as a board from his toes to his head.

Great-aunty Hauty and Grandpère Hy stood in front of the gangsters. They were dressed in their finest black silks. Great-aunty Hauty had purple plumes in her hat, as did Grandpère Hy.

"I DON'T EVEN KNOW WHY WE'RE HERE," said Grandpère Hy in a shout that he managed to whisper. "NO SUCH THING AS HARRY!"

"We're here because we're family!" hissed Great-aunty Hauty directly into his ear. "We have to humor them!" she whispered. "And besides, I do believe Mother made her delicious apple kugel for the get-together after the service." She nodded her head so hard, her plumes looked like the wings of a bird ready for takeoff.

"TUT," said Grandpère Hy. "YOU SHOULD HAVE

TOLD ME THAT. I WOULDN'T HAVE HAD SEC-
ONDS FOR SUPPER."

Yogurt Skunk stood behind everyone. He carried
the purple flower Clematis, who had begged to come.

"If I pluck you from your stem, you'll die," warned
Skunk.

"Harry was a Friend with a capital *F*," explained
Clematis. His teardrops kept his petals looking dewy.
"I want to be there for him."

Lulu stood before the group in attendance, with her
back to the Umbrella Tree. "Let us begin with a
prayer," she said.

All those assembled bowed their heads.

This was Lulu's prayer. "Oh, God, I don't know
what you're doing! I don't think *you* know what
you're doing! How could you let this happen! What

is the matter with you, anyway?" she boomed at the sky, her eyes piercing the clouds, seeking God for a face-to-face.

All those assembled gasped. They held their hands to their mouths, and their eyes grew wide in surprise and in fear. They looked all around, as if expecting the worst.

"I'm going to faint!" said Great-aunty Hauty.

"BETTER NOT, 'CAUSE I'M NOT CATCHING YOU IF YOU DO!" yelled Grandpère Hy.

"Lulu Atlantis!" Mother sputtered through clenched teeth.

"But it's the way I feel!" cried Lulu. "I want God to know. Why shouldn't God know?" she said, stamping her foot with the beat of each word.

"I'm sure he already does," said Mother quietly.

"Here, may I?" said the Eggman. He walked up to Lulu and took her hands in his. Lulu held her breath and gulped back huge lumps of tears. She squeezed her eyes tight and two thin tears trickled down her cheeks. She nodded to the Eggman and then stepped back to huddle as close to Mother as it was humanly possible to huddle.

Sam came over to Lulu and hugged her, burying his face in her tummy.

The Eggman cleared his throat, shot a quick glance at Mother and then said to everyone, "Harry was a friend not all of us could see. But just because everybody couldn't see him doesn't mean we didn't all learn from him. It seems to me that Harry taught us his lesson by *living* it. Harry stayed at Lulu's side through thick and thin, because he considered her his True Blue Friend. And Harry watched over Sam, not only because of his own love for him, but because of Lulu's love for her little brother. Harry was there for Lulu when she risked her own life to save her brother, her own True Blue Brother. This is the mark of True Blue Love: *being there*. Being there, without question and without doubt." The Eggman paused, turning to look directly into Lulu's eyes. He held out his hand to her. "That, Lulu Atlantis, is what True Blue Love is."

CHAPTER TEN

The field darkened as the sun lowered behind Black Mountain. Lights of fireflies flickered. Peepers chirped in the background. A thin, sharp crescent moon sliced through the clouds, so that the faces of Harry's mourners appeared to have been dipped in silver.

The group at the Umbrella Tree was silent. Then the gangsters nudged each other and grunted solemnly, finding solace and truth in the words of the Eggman. Mother picked up Sam and held him in one arm. She put her other arm around Lulu and drew her close, and she bowed her head to the Eggman.

Great-aunty Hauty and Grandpère Hy kissed each other softly on the cheek.

Yogurt Skunk put his hand over Clematis, to protect him from the gathering chill in the night air. Clematis, in Skunk's hand, drooped and withered.

The Eggman looked at the flower and said, "We'd better get that purple fellow into some water real quick."

Mother said to all those assembled, "Yes. Please, all of you, come back to the house, where there is apple kugel and coffee."

The group, a group honorable in number and in re-spect for the memory of a beloved spider, returned to Mother's house.

Lulu lurked behind. "I'll be there in a minute, Mother," she said.

Alone in the field, with only the occasional bit of song from a coyote or the short hoot of a barn owl, Lulu crawled beneath the Umbrella Tree. She sat cross-legged on the moist earth. She took off her top hat and placed it on the ground beside her knee.

Lulu looked at her knee. She pictured Harry perched there. She studied the folds of the pants of her tuxedo, picturing her best friend clinging to them, scuttling within them.

Lulu remembered all the things they had done.

"I wonder whatever happened to our Frog Prince," she said. She sniffled a sniffle.

And, "Remember the first time we saw Yogurt Skunk?" Lulu's throat ached with a huge, achy lump. She wiped her nose.

And, "How about that kitchen in the Gangsters' Bakery? That was some kitchen!" Lulu choked. She paused. She held her face in her hands, but she would not, *would* not . . . absolutely no way on earth would she allow herself to cry! She pushed at her eyes with the heels of her hands, forcing the tears to remain inside.

It was at this point, as she sat there holding back the tears, rocking back and forth, that Lulu began wondering. Please understand, wondering is a lovely thing to do when you are watching a snowstorm from your bedroom window, or listening to loons whistle up the lake. Wonder at grumbling rolls of thunder shaking the valley, and wonder at the glow of your baby brother's face alight to the constant magic of music. But never wonder while sitting alone under an umbrella mulberry tree, missing a lost friend. It leads to folly.

As she sat alone under the Umbrella Tree, mourning her friend, Lulu wondered, "Why am I so *stupid?* How did the Eggman learn lessons from Harry? How did Clematis learn such love from Harry that he's giving up his life for him? Why did Sam learn, and Mother learn . . . *but not me?*" Here Lulu choked back a sob. She cried, "All I've learned is how to be angry!

I . . . AM . . . SO . . . *MAD!*" Lulu shouted at the top of her lungs. She punched the earth with her fists.

She looked up to the sky through the twiggy ceiling of the Umbrella Tree. Once again, she yelled at God, "WHY DID YOU TAKE HIM AWAY FROM ME?" And then, as if yelling at God weren't enough, she yelled at Harry, "HOW COULD YOU LEAVE ME?" Lulu choked back tears.

"You coming?" Lulu heard the Eggman call from outside the Umbrella Tree.

"No."

"We'll miss you, Lulu Atlantis," he called through the wall of branches.

"Wait! What you said about learning from Harry," Lulu called through the tree to the Eggman. "Well, I *can't!* I'm too angry! Angry he left, and angry I wasn't a . . . b-b-better friend!"

"Lulu," the Eggman called softly back, "you were

the best friend that Harry could have had. Look at all you did—*for* him and *with* him. You always made sure Harry had a cool spot in your pocket in the summer and a warm spot in your mitten in the winter. You always made sure Mother didn't accidentally sweep away his cobwebs. Why, you rescued him from a pit of snakes! And together, you two braved the gangsters for the Secret Ingredient. You both fought monsters to protect people who weren't even nice to you." The Eggman's voice lowered. He said, "And your heart broke when you saw him go over Bear Foot Falls."

"Oh, oh," moaned Lulu. "I had it! I had True Blue Love all along, and I was too stupid to know it!"

The Eggman said, "You *still* have True Blue Love. Look at you and Yogurt Skunk, you and Mother, you and Sam." He grinned. "And what about me? If I were in trouble, wouldn't you help me?"

"Well . . . yes," said Lulu.

"And if any of us needed you, wouldn't you be there for us?" said the Eggman.

Lulu shrugged. "Yes," she whispered.

"Forever?"

"Forever."

"Well, isn't that what Harry taught us? *That's* what True Blue Love is."

"Y-y-yes," said Lulu. Her voice was choked with all those tears she was still holding in. "Oh, I'll miss Harry more than anything!"

There was silence for two seconds, then six and then ten.

And then another voice, an entirely different voice, said, "No, miss. Thanks to a certain spider's spinning skills and a cobweb quickly spun to a tree branch, you won't have to miss your Harry at all!" And a tiny top hat appeared on her knee.

Lulu shut her eyes tight.

"Nothing's impossible, I have found,
For when my chin is on the ground . . ."

Lulu still dared not open her eyes.

"I pick myself up, dust myself off . . ."

Finally, Lulu slowly opened one eye and then the other. She saw a frail, delicate creature, a tiny, dark being in a green jacket and a red bow tie, skitter onto her knee.

"It's me!" said a tiny voice.

It was then that Lulu *really* began to cry.

CHAPTER ELEVEN

Please understand, when I say cry, I really mean to say *weep. Bawl.* SOB. BLUBBER! **SQUALL!** And all the words in my thesaurus tell me this: Lulu literally *melted* into tears.

Lulu's shoulders shook and the hair surrounding her face became soaked. Her cheeks grew red and puffy and so did her eyes. Her chest heaved and her nose filled with snot. It ran down to her upper lip and she swiped at it with the sleeve of her borrowed tuxedo. Rivers of tears ran down the front of her tuxedo and pooled in puddles, then lakes, in her lap.

Harry hung on to her knee for dear life.

By the time Lulu made it back home, assisted by the Eggman, buoyed up by Harry's song (*"Work like a soul inspired/Till the battle of the day is won./You may be sick and tired,/But you'll be a man, my son!"*), she looked as if she'd been dragged around the fields by cows.

"Holy Toledo!" said Mother.

"My heavenly days!" said Great-aunty Hauty. "What a sodden mess you are, Lulu Atlantis. What with the tears and all!"

"Hello," said Harry quietly.

"Hello?" asked Yogurt Skunk.

"Hello?" asked Clematis, looking somewhat refreshed in a piece of crystal stemware filled with clear, cool water.

"Whatcha mean, hullo?" asked Jimmy Creamcheese.

"*HELLO!*" yelled Yogurt Skunk, racing to Harry and shaking all his hands.

There were those in the room who could not see Harry. But one look at the beaming face of Lulu Atlantis told them: "A miracle has happened! Harry is back!"

Oh, what a party they had! What started out as a funeral ended up a feast. The kugel, the grapes and cheeses and bits of dried bagel and crackers, the chocolate cake the gangsters had brought, and punch with rum and punch with no rum and Harry with his top hat and Lulu with hers! Oh, what conversations they had of the places where True Blue Love can take you and the feelings it can give you!

"Where else do you find such highs?" asked Lefty-Righty Louie.

"Where else do you find such lows?" asked Scarecrow, discovering that they were almost out of apple kugel.

Mother put on music. She turned and said, "May I have this dance, Harry?"

"Do you see me?" asked Harry.

Mother didn't answer. She smiled off into the air somewhere above his head. She held her hand out flat with the palm upward, as she had seen her daughter do so many times. She swung it gently back and forth, as if the hand were seeking something. Harry jumped aboard.

"All set!" he said.

Mother continued waving her hand gently. Lulu said to her, "You can start dancing now. Harry's in your hand."

"Of course he is! How are you, Harry, my dear?"

"Just fine, Mother. And how are you?"

But Mother was already busy humming and whirling about the living room floor in a grand Vienna waltz and didn't answer him.

Great-aunty Hauty danced with Chef Jimmy Cream-cheese.

"Do take your hat off when you're dancing with a lady," said Great-aunty Hauty.

"When I'm dancin' wit' a lady, I will!" said Chef Jimmy, and roared with laughter. (It must be noted, Great-aunty Hauty roared with laughter as well.)

Grandpère Hy beat time with his cane and ate from the banquet table with gusto.

The Eggman picked up Sam and set him on his shoulders. Then the Eggman bowed carefully to Lulu, making sure Sam did not fall.

"Dance, ma'am?" he said.

"Yes, thank you!" said Lulu. And she curtsied.

The Eggman danced Lulu around the floor as Sam bounced and rocked on his shoulders.

"Got any new stories for me?" said the Eggman, laughing.

"Isn't today's story enough?" said Lulu.

"You can tell me this story some cold winter afternoon. I'll be happy to hear a rehash of the past week's events. You're a great storyteller, Miss Lulu Atlantis!"

"It's a gift. I got it from my father," said Lulu.

CHAPTER TWELVE

As you watch the merrymakers making merry in the home of Lulu Atlantis, as you listen to them laugh and sing, as you count their numbers and recall their names, as you accompany them through this topsy-turvy turmoil of despair and happiness, of grief turning into glee, you may wonder, "Whatever happened to that cat? So where's Princess Fancy? Did she vanish into thin air?"

Please don't think I've forgotten her. I haven't! I can tell you this about Princess Fancy. As far as the cat went, that *feline*, that prickly-pawed, self-proclaimed princess, well! I will tell you what became of *her*:

> *Earth proved a mysterious place,*
> *With nothing to offer in gold,*
> *Neither ruby nor diamond to hold.*

Friendship was the jewel
Of the brave and the bold!
What's left but a marmalade sky?

Yes, Fancy returned to the skies,
Paws pushing past fireflies,
No thank-yous, no
simple good-byes,
A cat to a marmalade sky.

Her feet had golden boots,
Pinching at her toes.
Her golden earrings tarnished,
No diamond pierced her nose.
The circle at her forehead?
The red tattoo was gone.
A smudge of ash was in its place,
Colorless, woebegone.
Even princesses must pay

For meanness they have done,
By drifting back beyond the clouds,
Beyond the stars, the sun . . .

A Princess from another world,
A Princess! It was told
From a world with glitterflies
And oak trees made of gold;
It was hard . . . impossible!
To make her happy here.
The family that found
This feline
Had nothing more
To fear.

ALMOST THE END

CHAPTER LUCKY THIRTEEN

When the kugel platters contained only leftover crumbs and the coffeepots were almost empty, when the chill night air crept in through windowpanes and the moon was high in the sky, Lulu said to her guests, "Ahem! Harry and I would now like to perform a song and a dance for all those assembled."

Although Lulu still looked like a wet tissue, Harry told her, "You never looked lovelier!" And although Harry looked rather disheveled himself, Lulu said, "And you, Sir Harry, are as stylish and handsome as ever!"

Harry took several toothpicks from the table of food and used them as walking sticks. Lulu borrowed Grandpère's cane.

They did a very fine soft-shoe routine, and sang,

"Nothing's impossible, I have found,
For when my chin is on the ground . . .
I pick myself up, dust myself off,
Start all over again."

Everyone joined in and sang with them, and clapped their hands and grinned and rubbed each other's shoulders and hiccupped and grinned some more.

The glow of their smiles that night, the night of the end of heartache, the night of Harry's return, the night of the miracle of True Blue Love, could be seen through the windows of Lulu's house for miles around. That glow of the smiles of friends old and friends new warmed the cool night air, and it even outdid the silver shine of the moon.

THE END

About the Author

When Patricia Martin was a little girl, she had a best friend named Harry who happened to be a top-hatted daddy longlegs spider. These days, Ms. Martin lives with her husband; with her dogs, Harry and Poppy; and with her spiders in Bolton Landing, New York. She spends her time writing, chasing Harry and Poppy, and leaving her spiders blissfully alone.